Grim JUSTICE

ROYAL BASTARDS MC

TONOPAH, NV

USA *TODAY* BESTSELLING AUTHOR

NIKKI LANDIS

Table of Contents

CHAPTER 1 1

CHAPTER 2 9

CHAPTER 3 17

CHAPTER 4 25

CHAPTER 5 33

CHAPTER 6 41

CHAPTER 7 49

CHAPTER 8 55

CHAPTER 9 63

CHAPTER 10 71

CHAPTER 11 79

CHAPTER 12 87

CHAPTER 13 95

CHAPTER 14 101

EPILOGUE... 109

REAPER MÉTIER 119

TONOPAH, NV CHAPTER 123

LAS VEGAS, NV CHAPTER 129

PLAYLIST 133

6TH RUN... 139

SNEAK PEEK 163

ABOUT THE AUTHOR 187

AUTHOR'S NOTE

Royal Bastards MC
Tonopah, NV

Grim Justice is the continuing story of Grim, the President of the Royal Bastards MC, Tonopah, NV Chapter. There's revenge, torture, violence, biker slang, somnophilia, steamy scenes, fetal loss, references to abuse, and dark content.

You'll need to read *Devil's Ride* first. It's also highly recommended to read *Infinitely Mine*. The RBMC builds from one book to the next so the series is best enjoyed when read in order since ongoing stories overlap and characters appear throughout from start to finish.

A new motorcycle club will release in this supernatural world of bikers: the Night Striders MC, with president Undertaker, beginning with *Rebel Road*. Watch for more in 2025.

I'm also starting books in the Kings of Anarchy MC and Saint's Outlaws MC, both are shared world with fantastic authors. More to come!

And I'm also excited to announce a new universe titled Summit Hill that will crossover in the MC Romance, Asylum, Secret Society, and Serial Killer Romance genres.

If you love crossover stories, check out the Devil's Murder MC. The Tonopah Royal Bastards are close allies. The series begins with *Crow*.

ROYAL BASTARDS CODE

PROTECT: The club and your brothers come before anything else, and must be protected at all costs. **CLUB** is **FAMILY.**

RESPECT: Earn it & Give it. Respect club law. Respect the patch. Respect your brothers. Disrespect a member and there will be hell to pay.

HONOR: Being patched in is an honor, not a right. Your colors are sacred, not to be left alone, and **NEVER** let them touch the ground.

OL' LADIES: Never disrespect a member's or brother's Ol' Lady. **PERIOD.**

CHURCH is **MANDATORY.**

LOYALTY: Takes precedence over all, including well-being.

HONESTY: Never **LIE, CHEAT,** or **STEAL** from another member or the club.

TERRITORY: You are to respect your brother's property and follow their Chapter's club rules.

TRUST: Years to earn it...seconds to lose it.

NEVER RIDE OFF: Brothers do not abandon their family.

COMMON TERMS

RBMC Royal Bastards Motorcycle Club. One-percenter outlaw MC. Founded in Tonopah, NV 1985. Founded in Las Vegas, NV 2023.

Devil's Ride A deadly motorcycle ride into the Nevada desert and initiation into the club.

Reaper Demonic entity sharing the body of every Royal Bastard club member in the Tonopah chapter. A collector of souls at time of death.

Crossroads Bar & clubhouse owned by the RBMC Tonopah, NV chapter.

Pres President of the club. His word is law.

Brotherhood An unbreakable bond that trumps all other interpersonal relationships.

One-percenter Outlaw biker/club.

Ol' lady A member's woman, protected wife status.

Cut Leather vest worn by club members, adorned with patches and club colors, sacred to members.

Reaping Slang, killing those marked for death.

Church An official club meeting, led by president.

Chapel The location for church meetings in the clubhouse.

Prospect Probationary member sponsored by a ranking officer, banned from church until a full patch.

Full Patch A new member approved for membership.

Hog Motorcycle

Cage Vehicle

Muffler bunny Club girl, also called sweet butt, cut slut.

BSMC Bloody Scorpions MC, rival club to the RBMC.

Royal Bastards MC

Tonopah, NV Chapter

There's a peace that can only be found on the other side of war.
I've waited nearly two decades for justice.
And I'm finally close enough to get revenge.
The bad blood between me and Razr goes way back to the day his father, Scar, murdered my old pres, Keys.
I took out Scar and then Razr's brother, Acid. They paid for their crimes.
I won't rest until Razr meets the Reaper and faces judgment.

But the past carries secrets I never imagined.
New information surfaces and challenges everything I know.
It's not just about protecting my club.
I'll do anything to keep my ol' lady and my son safe.
I would even give up the throne to ensure they survive.
Because nothing will stop me from reaping Razr's soul and forcing him to his knees.
There's a reason I'm called Grim. Death is my playground.
I'll end this war and the feud with the Scorpions.
Not a soul, Reaper, or Lucifer himself will stop me.

ROYAL BASTARDS MC

Chapter 1

GRiM

"CHURCH IS IN SESSION," I growled, banging the skull-headed gavel on the wooden surface of the table. "Listen up."

Every member inside the chapel straightened in their seats, and more than one reaper pushed a little closer to the surface of the faces that watched with rapt attention. If I wasn't the grim fucking reaper and I didn't know the secrets we held, I might have been a little afraid of the ghostly, skeletal visages that stared my way.

But nothing much scared you when you already struck a bargain with the devil and wielded a scythe that reaped the darkest of souls. I wasn't afraid of death. I *was* death. The men in this room shared that morbid, powerful connection.

"Razr is out of prison," I announced, glancing at Mammoth, my V.P., who had yet to hear the news.

He arched a dark brow and sat back against his seat. "Fuck."

Yeah, fuck.

Until this moment, only Rael knew of Razr's release. I ordered him to keep it on lockdown since Mammoth married Rowen. Less than two fucking days for a honeymoon. I couldn't give him longer. I needed my V.P.

It wouldn't be the first time that the needs of the club trumped our personal relationships, and it wouldn't be the last. Every ol' lady understood the sacrifice she made when she supported her man. Did that mean we loved them any less? Fuck no. Every choice I made ensured the safety of our members and their families. Even if I had lacked in that department, our reapers would never have allowed it. They were obsessed, possessive, and overprotective when it came to our women. We often had to stifle the reapers' instincts because the demonic entities liked to fuck, fight, ride, and hunt. Rael's was the worst.

My Trish experienced the darkest aspects of MC life before we ever got serious. It almost broke us apart, but we fought every single fucking day to stay together.

"You should have told me sooner," Mammoth sighed.

"Not when you just got hitched, brother," Rael responded. "Pres wanted to wait. We fucking waited."

The left corner of Mammoth's lip lifted in a snarl. "Don't fucking piss me off, Rael."

Our S.A.A. and shit-starter shrugged. "Just sayin' the truth, old man. Besides, shouldn't you be happy after puttin' a ring on Rowen's finger?"

I shot Rael a look. He knew what the fuck he was doing. Crazy fucker got off on stirring the goddamn pot. He loved to fuck with Mammoth. "Knock it the fuck off, or you'll be cleaning the toilets after Mammoth shits."

Rael made a gagging sound. "I just threw up in my mouth a little."

"Grow the fuck up," Mammoth growled.

2

Christ.

Rael blew him a kiss.

"I swear to fuck," I began, "I am not in the mood for this shit."

"Just tryin' to keep things light, pres."

"Don't then," I hissed, turning to the rest of the members who had watched the exchange with humor.

We all knew how Rael acted when shit grew serious. He used humor to deflect because his reaper was an asshole. Also, because he cared as deeply about the club and its members as he did about his ol' lady Nylah and his twin sons, Gavin and Gage. He was my Sergeant at Arms because of his loyalty and dedication to the club. There was no obstacle that would prevent him from protecting our way of life, a brother, or an ol' lady.

Exorcist ticked his chin my way. "Tell us what you want, pres. No one wants to sit on this and allow Razr to make the first move."

"I vote we pay him a visit and end shit now," Wraith added.

My reaper agreed. "We hunt. Tonight."

"Vengeance," Hannibal shouted, pounding his fist on the table.

"Vengeance," I agreed. "For Keys and Lockjaw and all the brothers we've lost. For every fucking time we've had to lockdown this clubhouse and protect our families." A growl left my throat. "For the things we can't recover, and the time wasted, for the members no longer with us, and the cuts that hang as a reminder of our fallen brothers."

Thoughts of Trish and the baby we lost because of her stepbrother Moby and his vicious attack, the separation Razr caused, and the heartache—all the grief surfaced. I had to see him suffer.

My Reaper needed to reap his fucking soul.

Mammoth slammed his fist down, giving the room a wide grin. "Sharpen those scythes, brothers."

Rael tilted his head back and let his reaper howl. Actually, it was probably the berserker inside him. "I won't show mercy. The berserker won't allow it. Not with my Nylah and twins."

"I would expect nothing less."

"You're the Grim," he grunted. "The fucking Grim Reaper. We'll have our revenge, pres."

Yeah, we fucking would.

My gaze flicked around the room, taking in the framed leather vests that hung on the walls. A giant grim reaper, molded from steel, suspended on the farthest wall and loomed over us. In the middle of the table, a skull with a beard and crown had been etched into the surface, forever reminding us of our allegiance to the Royal Bastards MC. The patch that brought us all together and formed a sacred brotherhood.

"I can help."

I jolted, pushing back from the table as the men around me scattered. It wasn't fear that spurred on that reaction. We weren't afraid of what he could do because he fucked with us, but he didn't hurt us. The Reapers wouldn't allow it.

Of course, the asshole lounging in the center of the table in front of us could do whatever the fuck he wanted, and he often did. He just liked the element of surprise. The devil got off on that shit.

My gaze focused on him, watching as he sat there, right on our fucking emblem, and draped a hand over his knee.

Lucifer fucking Morningstar. I never trusted a word he spoke since the day I signed his contract in my blood. Lucifer always pushed his interests and agenda ahead of business. The only thing he liked more was his endless games.

I didn't have the time for his bullshit.

"You're interrupting church," I growled.

"Yes." He waved my words away like they were unimportant, and I felt my Reaper grow annoyed. "I came to offer my assistance."

Mammoth gave me a slight head shake. Rael grinned. It wasn't one of his teasing smiles. This was one of those dark grins that caused most people to cower in terror.

Sick. Twisted. Depraved. Downright sinful.

Lucifer lazily crooked a finger in Rael's direction. "Come play with me if you dare."

I didn't give Rael a chance to get worked up. "Enough. Why are you here?"

"As I said, to offer assistance." He swung his long legs over the table, slithering like a snake to the edge before hopping off.

I had to blink a few times to be sure I saw that right. His legs had become loose as spaghetti noodles and slightly wobbled, moving his body over the wooden surface with a tiny hiss.

As I stared, he stood, his body appearing normal—or as close as he would ever get to being human.

"Ah, yes. Down to business?" He glanced at Rael and winked. "Or not. Your choice."

"Business," I grunted, gesturing to a chair. "I assume you want us all present."

"I do."

No point in trying to end church until he vanished. He would leave when he was ready and not a fucking second before that.

"Why do we need your assistance?" I asked, taking my seat.

"I never said you *needed* it," he pointed out, lifting a bottle of whiskey from the table. He tilted the bottle toward his mouth and sucked the liquid from the amber glass. A forked tongue slid between his lips to lick the edge clean.

Fuck. I couldn't help the shiver that ghosted my spine.

A dark chuckle escaped as he sat back, snapping his fingers.

The bottle disappeared.

"Okay. Why are you offering?"

"Let's just say it's an attractive option."

For who? Him? I snorted. "I'm sure it is for you."

Rael snickered.

Mammoth shook his head. "You're toying with us. We all know it."

"Stop the games," I ordered. "Tell us what we need to know."

"It's no secret I have a vested interest in your success." He shrugged. "That was part of the agreement, Grim."

Yes. He never let us forget it. "And?"

"This is my effort to ensure things go smoothly."

Smoothly? Nothing ever went fucking smoothly with my club unless we let our Reapers free to harvest souls.

"You're telling us nothing," Wraith spat.

Exorcist cracked his neck. "I don't like where this is going."

I held up my hand to silence them. The added commentary would only piss off Lucifer. I really hated that he could manipulate us so effortlessly.

"Are you declining my assistance?"

Refusing his help? No. His interference? Hell yeah.

"It's hard to know how to reply when I don't have the knowledge to make a decision."

"Wise," Lucifer concluded. "You're the leader this club needed since Scar began this war. You have all the tools you require to end this feud."

Then why the fuck did he show up?

Frustrated expressions littered faces around the chapel.

Laughter spilled from Lucifer's mouth as he pushed to his feet. "Such a serious lot. Reapers never change."

Mammoth sneered in his direction. "We're exactly as you made us."

"True," Lucifer agreed, "at least partially. There's still that pesky bit about free choice and individual personality. Keeps things interesting."

I scrubbed a hand down my face and over my short beard. His visits were tedious and mentally exhausting. "And the point of this?"

"Whatever the fuck I want it to be," Lucifer hissed. A demonic, horned visage briefly flashed before his features returned to their handsome, flawless norm. The devil loved to appear in control, impeccably dressed, and always one step ahead of us.

His midnight tailored suit, bright white button-up shirt, and shiny black crocodile leather oxford shoes completed the look. He almost passed for a wealthy, self-absorbed businessman except for the sardonic grin and black nails that ended in sharp points. I had to give him credit for remaining as mysterious, unpredictable, and cocky as the day we first met.

The devil was a master, and we remained nothing more than pawns.

He reached out and gripped my shoulder, giving it a hard squeeze. "You never disappoint." His hand dropped. "When you need me, I'll be enjoying a walk in the desert."

Before I could reply, he fucking vanished. Just like I predicted.

"Motherfucker," Mammoth mumbled.

"That sick fuck enjoyed this," Rael added.

Lucifer's visit changed nothing. "Lucifer's games don't affect our choices. We have a murderer to bring to justice. Reaping his soul is all that matters."

Fists pounded the table in agreement as my brothers took to their seats.

My gaze flicked around the room, noting their determination. We would end this war and send Razr to hell, where he belonged—no more delays.

"Mammoth."

"Yeah, pres?"

"We still have that box of fireworks?"

A wicked smile curled the corners of his mouth upward. "We do."

"Rael?"

"Anything you want, pres, I can get it."

"Smoke bombs. A lot of them."

"No problem."

"Wraith?" I asked.

"Pres?"

"Feel like pulling a little disappearing act?"

Wraith could pass through walls. It was a handy trick.

"Sure. Always ready for a little ghostly action," he joked.

"Shadow?"

"Yeah?"

"Tell the shadows to be ready to play."

"It'll be a pleasure, pres."

Good. "I need everyone ready to leave at dusk."

Something in the room shifted. An unforeseen force that had seemed to bog us down now disappeared. Shoulders squared and backs straightened. Several nods followed my words. Tension fizzled. Eagerness sprang into the eyes of my brothers. This was a historic moment for the club.

"Church is dismissed," I announced, rising to my feet to slam the gavel down. "Tonight, we ride."

ROYAL BASTARDS MC

Chapter 2

GRiM

"*Y*OU FAMILIAR WITH THE *Grim Reaper? What he does?"*

Yep. "Like killing people with a scythe?"

He smirked. "You could say that. A true reaper harvests souls. He sends them to hell for eternity. It's the soul that matters." He knelt before me, careful not to get a speck of dust or sand on his suit.

"For you, I'll throw in a little something special. Auras are the true reflection of the soul. You want to know who's worthy of the Reaper's blade? The darkest souls. Those covered in ebony shadow."

The devil laughed and stood, snapping his fingers once more as a piece of parchment appeared out of thin air. An invisible pen began writing words in onyx ink quickly down the page, leaving two blank lines at the bottom.

He lifted his other hand and bit off the edge of his finger as blood dripped from the digit, and he signed the bottom line in his dark crimson blood. The wound healed immediately.

"Your turn."

He thrust the contract close enough that I could read the contents from top to bottom. A twisted smile curved my lips. I was bound to the individual who signed this contract. Lucifer Morningstar.

Given carte blanche, my only requirement was reaping souls and handing them to the devil to fulfill the contract. No specific number was written down, but explicit instructions for recognizing souls that were to be reaped.

If I failed to take out those marked, I'd violate his contract. Punishment could mean revocation of my abilities and immediate death. If that happened, my soul was Lucifer's. Either way, he won.

Brilliant. There was no way to trick the devil. He was a master of deception and had already proved it. Lucifer was ensuring he received exactly what he wanted. If I didn't sign his contract, he would simply find another soul that would. It wasn't complicated to understand.

"My club?" I asked, taking an unsteady breath.

"You will take the position that Keys wanted. The president of the Royal Bastards MC. The devil's instrument."

At the devil's urging, I took on a new identity to cement my leadership and allegiance to my club.

It wasn't hard to come up with a road name that instantly evoked fear. A name that perfectly described my transformation. I wanted vengeance, the suffering of my enemies, and the calculating ability to rain down hell upon those who deserved it. A name that symbolized the cold, hard bastard I'd become.

Grim, the Reaper.

I blinked, jarring into awareness as I realized I must have dozed off. Strange. I didn't remember closing my eyes. The last thing I did was enter my office and sit behind my desk, planning how to take out Razr tonight.

My gaze locked on the window and the setting sun. Fucking Lucifer. Another round won in his sadistic games. He purposely put me to sleep so I would remember the contract I signed and his requirements. Not like I could ever forget. That moment was burned into my memory, scarring it forever.

Knowing my club waited, I pushed from the desk and strode toward the door. When I opened it, I found Mammoth waiting.

"We're all ready."

I gave him a crisp nod. "Good."

We left The Crossroads, and I approached my bike. The same bike that belonged to my father, Raptor. A beauty that still ran as perfectly as she did when he bought her.

A long row of rumbling engines formed behind me as I sank onto the saddle. Pulling on my gloves, I settled, focusing on the task ahead. Blood would spill tonight.

As if Lucifer couldn't resist, a blood moon hung low and full in the sky, casting a scarlet hue over the horizon. Around us, the desert stretched for endless miles. Predators slowly began their nightly hunt, unaware that the deadliest of all would soon rumble down Hwy 95.

My Reaper rose to the surface, and I welcomed his presence. When he joined me, I knew his protection would prevent any injury or harm. That was the bargain struck by Lucifer. I reaped. The Reaper protected. It wasn't his only duty, but he never failed. Invincibility lasted only as long as his presence. When he receded, it went with him.

But I could call upon my Reaper anytime I wanted.

He felt my restless energy. The rage that still lingered as a result of Keys' death and the other brothers we'd lost.

The agony I kept behind locked doors because it was too painful to expose the loss I suffered with Trish.

He felt everything as keenly as I did.

I grew to love the vicious Reaper that intertwined with my soul. We were one thought and entity. There was a hunter's drive in his monstrous thirst for vengeance—a predator's stealth and sick enjoyment. I wanted my enemies to suffer and bleed, and so did my Reaper.

Which led us to this moment as a long line of bikes left The Crossroads. We narrowed down Razr's location and knew he had to be at one of three different compounds. It turned out we weren't wrong.

About half a mile from the Scorpions MC clubhouse, we stashed our bikes and made our way on foot. My guys spread out, surrounding the perimeter.

That was when I spotted Razr on his cell, arguing with someone. He sounded pissed.

Good. His day was about to get a hell of a lot worse.

Fucking Razr and his family had plagued me and my club for over twenty years. Razr's father Scar began this war when he took my old pres Keys and Lockjaw. They were tortured, beaten, and left to die. I couldn't save either of them. I'd been taken, too, but I managed to fight them off long enough to escape.

That was when Lucifer found me in the desert. One simple contract promising vengeance. I never hesitated to accept his offer or the presence of the Reaper. When I took my place as the new president for the Tonopah, NV, chapter of the Royal Bastards MC, I did it with one goal: to avenge my fallen brothers and the man I loved like a father. Keys' death set in motion a chain reaction of events that included murder, mayhem, blood oaths, and hatred. A war that would only end when the last of Scar's bloodline had perished.

Razr was a dead man. He wouldn't escape the Reaper.

The club had gotten a little justice with Scar and Acid's deaths, but after all the shit with Razr, it wouldn't be settled until he was in the ground. Or, preferably, suffering eternal torment in hell. I'd be fucking happy to send him to Lucifer.

I'd come close to taking out Razr on multiple occasions and lost a couple of good brothers along the way. Several cuts were framed and hung in the chapel. Keys, Lockjaw, and Vector all had a place of reverence on the wall. Each man was a casualty in the war with the Scorpions. Raptor's cut was up there, too. He didn't die because of Scar or his sons, but another rival had taken him out when I was young. Another casualty in the endless war we seemed to wage since the club's conception in Nevada—at least, our chapter.

We'd paved the way with blood, and it never fucking ended.

Those framed cuts were a reminder nothing was permanent. Even with our Reapers, we weren't invincible.

My old man Raptor died when I was only twelve. He'd been a big part of the Royal Bastards and the SAA. I swore that once I was old enough, I would join the club my father loved and died for. I'd carry on his legacy.

There wasn't any other choice for me. It was my destiny to wear the skull and crown of the club, proudly giving my loyalty to the brotherhood. I'd die for that patch.

And I didn't hesitate to get the retribution we needed.

We never had a reason to use those smoke bombs or fireworks. Wraith didn't have to enter the compound. Shit went down fast once we approached the gate.

I didn't waste time. "Razr."

His gaze narrowed. "What the fuck do you want?"

That was an odd reaction. "Your surrender."

He scoffed. "Get the fuck away before I rain down bullets on your idiotic skull."

My Reaper chuckled. I let him out to play.

"Wrong choice."

Razr's eyes widened. "What the fuck are you?"

"Judgment."

He took a few steps back, hollering for help.

Pathetic.

I hovered off the ground, gripping my scythe. Around me, I felt the presence of my brethren. We formed a circle of death that stretched around the outer gate. No one would escape.

For so long, I dreamed about dragging out Razr's suffering. I wanted him to feel pain for days, or even weeks, before he died, and his soul was sent to Lucifer.

Now, I just wanted it over.

Bloody Scorpions MC members rushed from their clubhouse with guns, thinking they could harm us.

Dark laughter echoed around me.

"It's time to harvest."

We left no one alive. Screams filtered into the hot night air, rising into a cloudless dark sky. Stars populated in a giant sea of onyx, twinkling above.

When I separated Razr's soul from his body, I held him in the air, watching him tremble with fear. "You will die. Payment for your sins."

"Please," he begged. "You have the wrong—"

I cut him off, ripping into his oily, inky soul. So foul. As evil as I knew it would be. Lucifer would enjoy him for all eternity.

His cries fell on deaf ears. With a sharp cut, I slashed through the last of his essence, grinning when I saw it sucked into the earth, sinking into the pits of hell that opened to welcome him.

There was a part of me that thought this was too fucking easy. He'd gone down way too fucking fast with hardly any resistance. Almost like he didn't know who we were or why the fuck we hunted him down. Fucking ridiculous.

I didn't care what his thought process had been. He couldn't be allowed to live after all he'd done. We got our retribution and vindicated the men we lost. It was a good fucking day.

When the sun rose in a few hours, it would be a fresh start.

And I couldn't fucking wait to begin this new chapter of my life with Trish, expand our family, and discuss the future of the Tonopah Royal Bastards MC with my brothers.

ROYAL BASTARDS MC

Chapter 3

GRiM

"D_{EX?}"

TRISH'S SOFT VOICE pulled me from a deep sleep. I hadn't rested like this in so long I'd forgotten how energized I would feel when I woke. Every part of me felt invigorated. No dark thoughts to weigh me down. No worries.

The freedom of that weight and burden had been lifted with Razr's death, the last threat against the club and my family.

I planned to fucking enjoy every moment.

"Yeah, baby?"

I reached for her as she lifted off the mattress to drape her sexy body over my chest. Motherhood agreed with her. I'd always thought Trish was beautiful, but after Creed's birth, her hips had widened a little, and her breasts had grown fuller.

There was a slight roundness to her belly that I fucking adored. She'd given me so fucking much.

"You know you're stunning, don't you?" I murmured, tugging her higher until our mouths nearly touched.

A sweet smile curved her lips. "Flattery will get you lucky," she teased. "You don't have to say those things to me. I know how you feel."

"Babe, you need to get used to this. I'm never gonna stop telling you how gorgeous and perfect you are to me."

"You're such a flirt."

I leaned in and sucked her bottom lip into my mouth, nibbling on the pillow-soft flesh until I kissed her.

"Or maybe you're motivated by this." Her hand cupped my crotch. "Yeah, I think so." She moved her palm before I could grind into it.

Such a tease. The Reaper loved it.

My hands slid over her shoulders, down the delicate arch of her back to grip her luscious ass. "Angel, you can have all of me every fucking second of the day. This cock is yours."

"I'm aware." Her fingers rose and gently tugged on my beard. "Any chance I could convince you to rub this between my thighs?"

I didn't reply, picking her up and laying her back against the sheets so fast she squealed.

"Dex!"

At this moment, I couldn't be happier my woman slept naked. I dove into her center, pushing her hands away. "Spread wide for me, baby."

Trish's legs fell open, and I slid my tongue across her inner thigh, trailing kisses to her soft pink pussy. My beard rubbed skin along the way, and she shivered. Trish was already glistening, so I didn't hesitate to slide a finger inside her.

I could smell her arousal. My Reaper knew her musk so well I could find that intoxicating aroma anywhere she went, tracking her down if needed.

"God, Grim, you always know exactly what I need."

Her hips lifted as she moaned.

"I don't think you're full enough yet." Plunging a second finger into her depths, I slowly began to pump them in and out as I licked through her slit. *Always so fucking tight.* Finding the hood of her clit, I swiped upward with my tongue.

"Yes, just like that."

I gave her what she wanted, increasing the pace until she writhed beneath me.

"Dex. Shit."

"What do you need, baby?"

"You."

"Not specific enough," I teased.

"Your big fat cock!"

Knowing she wanted me with the same reckless desire I wanted her did wicked things to my body. Her cries sent an adrenaline rush to my brain as she reached out, grasping for air as I leaned back and swiped my hand across my mouth. *Delicious.*

"You're gonna take this dick, beautiful, and you're gonna come hard when I fuck you."

"Oh, God."

"Is that what you want?" I didn't wait for a reply. My hips snapped forward as I entered her, slamming home as a deep groan rose through my chest. That first plunge was always the fucking best. Nearly as euphoric as when I came.

Trish dug her nails into my arms as I watched her tits bouncing, driving into her wet cunt as she gripped me like no woman ever had. Every undulation of my hips drove me deeper. She grew wetter, softer, and yet somehow tighter.

I didn't expect her to come as quickly as she did.

Her channel squeezed my dick, and I had to thrust hard to remain inside her pussy. She spasmed around the girth, tightening those fluttering muscles around my shaft.

My body stilled as she writhed beneath me.

"Kiss me, Dex."

I could never deny her. My mouth captured the sweetest lips.

"I love you," she whispered as we parted.

My body demanded I move, staying still far too long as my dick throbbed. I slowly withdrew and glided back in, repeating the process until I was riding her hard, sweat clinging to my back.

"Mama? Daddy?"

Oh. Fuck. I froze mid-thrust.

Trish's eyes widened. "Creed."

There was one thing that could deflate a man's hard-on so fast it gave him blue balls. His child waking up early from a nap. I pulled out and rolled over, throwing an arm over my face. "Fuck."

I just got cockblocked by my two-year-old son.

Trish giggled. "Your cock is shriveling."

No shit. "I blame the baby monitor."

"You're the one who insisted we buy it."

She was right. "I still hate it."

"Oh, Dex." Soft laughter reached my ears as she kissed my cheek. "I'll get him."

"No," I sighed. "We'll both go. He'll get pissed if I'm not there."

"Alright. I'm going to get dressed."

I moved my arm in time to see her sexy naked ass jiggle before she pulled on a pair of underwear. She was much faster at this than me.

Maybe it was all the breastfeeding nights before she weaned Creed. I scooted off the bed and pouted, throwing on a pair of jeans. My flaccid dick looked pathetic as I stuffed it into my pants and zipped up.

Trish gave me an appraising look as I caught her gaze. She swept over my chest, down my stomach, and lingered on my dick. "I'm a lucky woman."

"Not fair. I have the worst luck in the world," I joked.

"Aw, baby. I'll make it up to you later."

"Blow job?" I asked with hope.

"Yeah. I'll swallow every drop, too."

Jesus. Christ. Blood traveled south and swelled my cock. "I can't go see my son until you make me think of something else."

She bit her lip. "Rael's naked ass?"

Ugh. That did it. Any hope of an erection faded.

"We're good now," I informed her as I gagged.

"I figured."

"Mama! Daddy! I want up!"

Creed wasn't waiting any longer.

Being the president had its perks, including having most of this floor and the apartment all our own. Creed slept in the next room, and the baby monitor didn't hesitate to announce his happy voice as he called out.

"Daddy! Grrrr."

"He just growled at me," I laughed, reaching for Trish's hand and leading her to Creed's room. I slowly pushed the door open, grinning at my boy as he bounced on his toddler bed. With his right arm, he clutched a stuffed brown bear to his chest. Cuddles.

The bear had a history. Trish gave him to me the day we met.

Her parents had struck my motorcycle when I passed out on the road, disoriented from a clandestine meeting with Lucifer Morningstar. A newly formed Reaper, I didn't have a clue how my life changed yet. She was the first person I saw after my ability as an Aurabarer awakened.

I was totally out of it when she approached. Didn't remember shit until I woke up with her standing over me, lying on the ground in the middle of the highway as a little girl with blonde curls showed kindness to a bloody, injured young man.

Now, all these years later, Creed slept with the bear and loved it. Never went anywhere without the toy either. He got pissed when we forgot it. The kid had my temper.

As we approached, I sniffed the air, catching the worst smell known to humankind. Trish nearly collided with me. My gaze swept over my son, landing on his free hand that was now trying to jam down the back of his diaper.

"Hu-ahh," I choked, turning my head.

"Dex," Trish admonished.

"I can't," I managed to reply, gagging a second time. "I'm gonna puke, babe."

"Daddy!" Creed shouted. "Poo!"

Yeah. Poo. Nasty as fuck. No one ever prepared you for the fact that your sweet little child actually shit like a man at two years old before he could potty train. Christ.

"Hu-ahh," I hacked, tasting bile.

Trish smacked my arm. "Stop."

"Babe, it's not possible." I turned my head, refusing to look at my son.

"I need you to pick him up and take him to the bathroom," she announced as she walked toward Creed, checking him over for the extent of the damage. "It's a bad blowout."

Blowout. Son. Two words that I never wanted to associate together ever again.

I sucked in air, gaining too much of Creed's odor at the same time, and slapped a hand against the nearest wall. "Can't do it, babe."

She turned to me, and I swear to fuck my woman glared.

This fierce side of her grew stronger after my son's birth, so I knew motherhood caused it, but she was almost fucking scary.

"Dexter Lanford. Get your ass over here. Now."

"Babe," I choked again, clearing my throat.

"You are the grim reaper. You've reaped dark souls. There's no way a two-year-old child's bowel movement is going to harm you."

She was right. I couldn't pussy out on this.

I squared my shoulders back and marched toward my son. All my good intentions vanished when he lifted his hand covered in poo and reached for me. Even my fucking Reaper receded. I felt him cower and hide. *For fuck's sake.*

It was just a little poop. Right?

I could power through this. Game fucking on.

Chancing a glance at my woman, the love of my life, and my son's mother, I experienced true terror when I caught her expression. My dick almost shriveled. Did I ever need sex again? Not sure.

"Daddy."

My chin dropped, and I saw total adoration in my son's gray eyes, which were the same shade as mine. Fuck yeah. I'd have ten more like him, even with all the stinky poo and blowouts.

Plastering a wide grin on my face, I scooped him up, ran to the bathroom, and walked into the shower, fully clothed. If I thought Trish could dress fast, it was nothing compared to how quickly I stripped myself and Creed down to nothing. Our naked asses were out there for my woman to see as I finally started the shower.

Creed loved to take baths or showers with Daddy. We had this perfected. I washed him first, then moved onto my body, thoroughly cleansing us both from any remaining poo.

"Daddy? What's this?"

He poked my fucking dick.

I jolted. Blinking, I lowered to his level, squatting so we could see one another eye to eye. "That's my penis, son. You have one, too. Remember?"

His eyes widened like he had forgotten, and I reminded him. Little fingers reached for his penis and tugged on it. "I'm like daddy."

"You're my boy," I agreed. Someday, the ladies would love him. He got his father's DNA in that department.

"Dex," Trish laughed. "He's still tugging on it."

"Well, he's curious." I dropped a kiss on top of Creed's wet hair. "This boy is all mine."

She snorted. "Don't I know it."

"My belly is rumbly," Creed announced, already forgetting about his appendage and focusing on his mother.

"Dry off with Daddy, and we'll go for a snack."

I helped Creed towel off and handed him over to Trish. She carried him from the bathroom, heading into his room for clean clothes and a diaper. My kid had zero interest in potty training. He'd sit in his own stink before he'd plop down on a kid's potty. We bought him one, and he shook his head, refusing to try. It stared back at me as I dressed, gloating as it glistened bright white, unused.

I flipped it off before joining Trish and Creed.

ROYAL BASTARDS MC

Chapter 4

TRiSH

"DON'T FORGET FAITH IS flying in today," I reminded Dex. "I need you to pick her and Jessa up."

My sister lived in Ohio. She left Nevada long before the drama with our father and my stepbrother Moby could harm her. Faith met and married a Marine. They had Jessa one year after they married. Everything about her life was perfect, from her beautiful home to her amazing husband and her precious daughter.

I wasn't jealous of her life, but I had been envious in the past. Those were dark days. The months after Moby beat me, and I miscarried Grim's baby. A time when I thought we'd never find our way back to one another. The war with the Bloody Scorpions MC and Razr had taken a toll on our relationship. Just when I thought I lost him forever, fate gave us one last chance.

I couldn't be happier now with my son and the man I loved.

"I remember," Grim answered, poking his head through the doorway as I made our bed. "Plane comes in at two p.m."

"Yes. Thanks, babe."

"Of course." He walked in and kissed me, smacking my ass before he headed out the door. "Love you, angel."

"Love you more."

"Impossible."

A smile stretched across my face as I finished fluffing the pillows on the bed, tackling a basket of laundry next. Creed's blowout two days earlier caused a massive cleaning spree in his room. Luckily, he didn't touch many of his toys, just the bedding, wall, and his body. I managed to finish most of the things on my list before my son's voice spilled through the monitor.

"Mama! I'm up!" Creed announced as I heard him bouncing on his toddler bed.

He was such a good boy. He never left his room when he woke up, even though he could turn knobs and open them. It scared me that he'd try one day, so Grim had installed a deadbolt and a chain on our apartment suite's door. I latched it at night as a precaution. If Creed ever roamed through the rooms, he couldn't get hurt. I babyproofed all of them before he was born.

Even Grim kept his things high up and out of reach, using drawers my son couldn't open. Guns and knives were locked up. We had latches on every cabinet. My son's curiosity would never place him in danger here.

When I approached his door, I heard him talking. Creed often spoke to himself. Maybe he liked the sound of his voice. His little imagination went wild when he played with his toys. He frequently put his little plastic superheroes to sleep or placed them in timeouts for being naughty. So creative.

I paused, leaning against the wall to listen.

"No. Grrrr."

That was new. I couldn't figure out what he meant when he made that growling sound.

Sometimes, he would laugh, and I had no idea what was going on in his little brain or what ideas were forming.

"Grrrr," he repeated as the bed made squeaking noises. "Sleepy for you."

When Creed said the word *sleep*, it sounded like *sēp*.

"Shhh. You go nigh-night."

I peeked into the room. Grim decorated it with a motorcycle theme—shocker. He spent a small fortune on the toddler bed, which had wooden side rails painted like a Harley with spinning wheels. Colorful motorcycle-shaped pillows in shades of green, red, and blue had fallen to the floor. The sheets and comforter matched. Creed loved having a bike like Daddy.

He held up his bear and hugged him before placing him in the middle of his bed. "Grrrr."

Maybe my son was making bear noises. Cute.

I entered his room, and he slid off the mattress, running toward me as I reached down and scooped him into my arms.

"Huggies."

"Huggies," I confirmed, squeezing him as he laughed. "Are you hungry?"

"Yes!"

"How about some fruit and oatmeal?"

Creed rubbed his stomach. "Yum!"

I carried him into our little kitchen area and placed him in his booster seat at the table. Once he was secure and had a bowl of Cheerios, I made his fruit and oatmeal. Our morning routine sped by in a blur. We watched a few Scooby-Doo movies and played with his toys. After lunch, I placed him down for a nap.

When I finally dropped into a chair, it was almost two. My eyes slid shut as I yawned. No one ever told me how exhausting it was to be the mother of a young child. Of course, I saw that firsthand with my sister, my best friend Sasha and her son Maverick, and some of the other ol' ladies and children of club members. Still, until you experienced parenthood yourself, you didn't have a clue.

I wouldn't trade this for any amount of money, though. After the miscarriage, I worried I would never have a baby. A lot of sleepless nights and nightmares followed that horrific loss. But now I had Creed, my beautiful boy, and I loved him more than I ever thought possible.

Keys jangled inside the lock on the apartment door, and I jolted awake on my feet in an instant. A bit disoriented, I realized I must have fallen asleep. One glance at my phone confirmed I had taken about an hour's nap. I smoothed my clothes and walked toward the door as it opened.

My sister's bright smile greeted me as Jessa rushed inside.

"Auntie Trish!"

"Hi, doll baby. Oh, wow! You've grown so much since I last saw you."

Jessa beamed a grin. "Where's Creed?"

"He's napping."

"Creed!" Jessa shouted, running toward his room.

"Jessa!" Faith admonished, but her little blonde twin had already run inside Creed's room. Faith and her daughter looked so alike that it was like stepping back in time to see my sister at that age.

"It's fine. He was due to wake up any minute."

Faith held out her arms for a hug, and I nearly tackled her. "I've missed you."

"Me too. I'm glad you're here."

My sister planned to stay for two weeks—a perfect visit.

"Trish, I'm gonna run and pick up some pizzas. You all need anything?"

I hardly noticed Grim as he stood at the door, watching us. Of course, he was the one who unlocked it. "Salad mix and ranch."

"What about you, Faith?"

"Anything zero sugar to drink. Milk for Jessa if you don't have it."

"Got it. I'll pick up another gallon. Creed loves milk, too." He strolled forward and popped a soft kiss on my lips. "Back in a few, beautiful. Leave the luggage. I'll take care of it when I come back."

"Thanks, babe."

Faith had arrived with several suitcases, a carry-on bag, and her purse. It was no small task traveling with a child.

After Grim left, we settled on the couch. "How long is Jim on ship for this time?"

"Nine months. It's so long. Jessa really misses him."

"And you?" I couldn't imagine taking that long of a break from Grim.

"I miss him too. But we make up for it when he's home," she laughed. "I'm pregnant. Just found out before he left."

"Oh, wow! Congrats!" I tugged her into another hug as she laughed.

"I'm thrilled. Hoping it's a boy this time."

"Boys are wonderful. A handful, but fun. At least until they dig into their diaper." I explained about the poo incident and the blowout to Faith, describing Grim's reaction in detail.

"Oh my God," she laughed, clutching her sides. "My cheeks hurt. That's hysterical."

"I swear he nearly got sick. Funniest thing ever," I agreed.

"Jim has gagged before, too. He tries to act like it doesn't faze him because he's a Marine. Jessa just got out of that stage, and now we'll dive back into it soon."

We both dissolved into giggles.

"The kids are awfully quiet," Faith observed.

She was right. I stood, and my sister followed. We approached the room and peeked inside.

While we were talking, Jessa managed to find her pink tea set and brought it to Creed's room. They had cleared off one of Creed's Lego tables and arranged the cups, saucers, and teapot on the surface, seating stuffed animals, including Cuddles, around them.

Creed held onto a cup and pretended to drink from it.

"You have to hold out your pinky, Cree."

She never said the last letter of his name.

He mimicked her, lifting his chin like she did.

"Now we sip tea and smile and pretend to be rich."

Faith snorted.

I couldn't hold back a giggle. Kids were so unpredictable.

Later, after pizza, we spent the evening catching up as the kids played. Creed loved having his cousin Jessa stay with us. We made plans to take the kids to Millie's Diner for breakfast and shopping the following day.

After I set up Faith and Jessa in the spare bedroom, I stripped and slipped under the covers, opening my tablet to read before Grim came to bed. I knew he was playing pool downstairs and would likely be up late. He wanted to give me space with my sister, and I appreciated his willingness to provide us with girl time.

Halfway through a chapter, my phone alerted me to an incoming call. The ID registered the call as spam. Ignoring it, I went back to my book. Five minutes later, it rang again. This time, the ID came up as unknown.

Frowning, I wondered who was calling. Could it be important? I decided to answer, swiping across to open the call. "Hello?"

Silence.

"Hello?" I repeated.

I heard a click. The call ended.

Weird.

My eyes grew heavy as I rolled onto my side. I turned off the volume and placed it beside me in case Grim called or texted.

My phone vibrated in my hand as my eyes snapped open. I'd fallen asleep for another fifteen minutes. Another incoming call from an unknown number.

I swiped across, answering before anyone could say a word. "This isn't funny."

Someone panted on the other end of the line, breathing heavily as if they just finished running a long distance.

"Rael? Is that you? Nylah will kick your ass."

Sometimes, Rael drunk-texted or called the wrong person. He dialed me more than once instead of his woman. She thought it was hilarious when it happened.

No reply. More breathing.

Another click. The call ended.

By now, I was annoyed. I decided to place the phone on my dresser where it wouldn't bother me when a new call flashed on the screen. No spam or unknown number. This time, it was someone I knew. A *dead* someone.

Moby. My stepbrother.

What the hell? Who was messing with me?

I refused to answer and threw my phone across the room. It skidded over the rug in front of Grim's dresser. For the next hour, it rang every five minutes. No voice mail.

I couldn't figure out how someone had Moby's phone. Grim destroyed it when he reaped Moby's soul. After Moby kidnapped me, he went after Grim. It didn't end well for my stepbrother.

Did someone new have his number? Did it go to a random person who thought I was someone else? Probably. This was just a case of mistaken identity. Creepy, but it had nothing to do with me.

I slid from the bed, powered off my phone, plugged it in to charge, and climbed back into bed. Tomorrow was a new day, and I closed my eyes, slipping into a peaceful rest.

ROYAL BASTARDS MC

Chapter 5

GRiM

IF YOU HAD TOLD me twenty years ago that I would end up the Grim Reaper, I would have laughed. And if you said I would stand face to face with Lucifer Morningstar, the devil himself, I'd have thought you were crazy. Life had taken drastic turns from where I began, twisting and looping in a long, dangerous, heartbreaking road before it finally smoothed out.

I wouldn't change a thing, though—not my club, my woman, my son, or the broken path that led me to this moment.

"All up in your feelings, huh, pres?" Rael asked, taking a seat on the empty stool on my left.

Mammoth sat down on my right. "Sure, he is. We finally reaped Razr's soul, and now he's fucking bored."

I snorted. "Yeah, that's it."

Rael slapped me on the back. "I'm sure I can find trouble for us to get into."

"Don't fucking think about it," I warned.

He shrugged and lifted his hands. "Fine. A drink, then?"

I already had a beer in front of me, but whiskey sounded damn good. "Yeah."

Mammoth gestured to the club girl behind the bar, a buxom blonde. Becca had been with us for years. She served the club members well, but I knew it wouldn't be long before she took off. Some already had. With members snatching up ol' ladies and starting families, the pool of single men had dried up. In truth, I didn't want all the free pussy and bare ass around the club much anymore. Parties? Sure. But beyond that? No.

I needed to speak to Snooki and see what she thought.

"My Reaper feels sad," Rael announced as I tossed back the shot Becca pushed my way.

Mammoth smirked. "You'll just have to spend more time with Nylah and your boys."

"Yeah, but reaping souls is fucking fun."

"You act like there aren't plenty of fucked up people in the world for us to send to Lucifer."

"I suppose there is. Didn't think of it like that," Rael mused.

"Or think at all," Mammoth teased.

"I just like death, murder, mayhem. Sue me."

My Reaper loved all those things, too. He just loved Trish more. But that call to wield a scythe always lingered.

There was something peaceful and satisfying about death. A tranquility that couldn't be obtained until the soul's release from the body. Morbid but true. The finality of the whole experience was downright addicting when you held all the power.

My brothers and I reaped souls because it was our duty, but our Reapers enjoyed separating the dark, curling tendrils of corruption that tried to hide from us.

Almost every soul we encountered tried to fight it in the end. Silly. You couldn't fight off a Reaper. A sinister shadow hovered over those who chose to harm others, specifically rapists, pedophiles, and murderers. Lucifer wanted those souls the most. He thrived on the essence of the wicked.

"All of us do, Rael," I reminded him.

Mammoth poured us all another shot. "But I feel my Reaper wanting to settle. He loves Rowen and Jakey. I think he wants to enjoy peace for a bit."

Rowen's son Jacob had special gifts, including the ability to see into the future through his artistic drawings. At only six, he showed potential to become a badass Reaper one day.

"Mine too," I admitted. "I think most of us have reached that point."

Rael seemed disgruntled. "I don't know. I can fuck Nylah, raise my boys, and still have plenty of time for unleashing carnage and my Reaper."

Yeah, that didn't surprise me.

"It's the berserker inside you. He's fucking nuts."

"Or you're just looney toons," Mammoth snickered.

Rael grinned. "Maybe all of the above. Crazy. The Berserker. Bored. Restless."

Mammoth gripped his shoulder and squeezed. "It'll be okay, brother."

"I know."

"We're in the business of harvesting souls, and there's no shortage," I reminded him.

Souls were our currency. A bargain struck with the devil and signed in our blood. I was the first, but new Reapers in the Tonopah chapter had increased our membership, pushing close to twenty. And we needed new prospects. I planned to ask Zane if he had friends who loved to ride. Wraith's son was a ballbuster like his old man. Handy to have around.

Zane would patch in soon and learn the secrets we kept—a burden we didn't trust to just anyone. You had to have grit, loyalty, and tenacity. Qualities not all men possessed. I could always pick the ones that did as soon as I met them.

Courtesy of Lucifer's gift, of course. He ensured I knew which souls had Royal Bastard potential and which ones needed to go to ground. Evil couldn't hide, and neither could the light. You couldn't have one without the other—nature's balance.

One thing Lucifer had zero control over. That must piss him off.

My chuckle drew Rael and Mammoth's attention.

"What's so funny?" Rael asked.

I told them what I'd been thinking about, how Lucifer didn't have the ability to control everything.

Mammoth shook his head. "I bet he would debate that."

Yeah, he would.

"I've spent so long planning vengeance and hating Razr that I'm almost disappointed it's over."

My V.P. nodded. "I hear you."

"That's what I'm sayin'. It's why my Reaper is still antsy."

I turned to Rael with a frown. "It's weird to still feel this way. I didn't expect it."

"We're sure he's dead, right?"

"Yeah, Mammoth, he's dead. We reaped his fucking soul. All of us. You don't survive that shit."

"I know." He rubbed the back of his neck. "Why do I still feel off? Like shit ain't sorted?"

"If all three of us are getting the same vibe, something is wrong. Maybe we didn't get all those Scorpions. You'd think they would run scared after we took out their pres and most of their chapter in Nevada."

"But the fuckers are like cockroaches, impossible to exterminate."

"I think we need to take a ride," I announced, "and find out if any of those vermin are hiding and plotting against us."

We headed toward our bikes, riding out as my V.P. and S.A.A. flanked me.

TRISH WAS ALREADY ASLEEP when I entered our room. The dim light silhouetted her body, and I couldn't wait to feel her warmth and soft curves.

I started emptying my pockets, stashing my gun and knife in the lockbox before stripping my clothes. My cut draped over the back of a nearby chair. Kicking off my boots, I dropped them with a soft thud onto the rug beside the bed. My wallet, keys, and smokes rested on top of my dresser.

Everything in its place.

Trish mumbled in her sleep and rolled onto her stomach. The blanket pulled from her body and exposed the slim, delicate arch of her back. My gaze followed the curve to the slope that led to her ass. Two delicious mounds that beckoned for my lips.

A devious smile curved my lips as the Reaper surfaced.

One of our favorite fantasies rose to mind. One that Trish enjoyed, too. It was a delicate art, fucking her while she slept, bringing her to the brink of an orgasm as she woke with a moan.

Now that I thought of it, the Reaper took control, prowling closer to the bed. I knelt on the mattress and kept my movements slow. Carefully, I tugged the remainder of the blanket from her body.

Her naked ass, thoroughly exposed, did wicked things to my brain. Would she like it if I played with her puckered hole at the same time that I entered her?

I moved closer, gently pushing her right leg higher as my fingers touched her knee, adjusting her so that Trish's pussy was at the perfect height. Down to my boxer briefs, I positioned myself behind her, noting she already appeared wet and ready even in her sleep.

Did she read a naughty book? Think of me as her eyes closed?

I freed my cock, stroking down the length from base to tip. Within a couple of pumps, I was hard and fully erect.

Fuck. It felt good, but I knew she would feel even better.

Trish's smooth skin and silky slit snared my attention to such a degree that I probably wouldn't notice if the entire world burned down around us. I was that lost to my woman.

Leaning between her open legs, I notched the crown of my cock at her entrance. My fist wrapped around my shaft, and I almost shuddered when a drop of pre-cum glistened at the tip.

No longer willing to wait, I pressed into her, still holding my cock firmly as I withdrew. My hips began to rock as I penetrated her, gliding in and out of her tight pussy. Even after having Creed, she still gripped my dick and sucked me into her body. That feeling was fucking addicting.

My grip on her hips tightened. Possessiveness swelled inside me, and the feral need to fuck almost overcame me.

The Reaper wanted her to scream my name. I couldn't risk hurting her. This was all about pleasure.

I pulled out as a shaky breath escaped my lungs, plunging back in, unable to get enough.

Trish gasped and moved her arms beneath her, pushing up slightly as I slid out, allowing her to position properly on her hands and knees. Like this, I would be able to drive deep, just how she liked it.

"Dex," she breathed. "I need more."

My hips snapped forward as I slammed inside her, roughly taking her now that she was awake. Gripping her ass, I pulled her back onto my cock with every thrust. I knew she enjoyed it when her fingers bunched the sheets and twisted the material in her hands.

"That's it, baby. Take this cock and fucking come."

Our skin slapped together. Our bodies collided.

Every time we fucked, it was better than the last. I didn't think my need for her would ever fade away. She possessed me, owned me, and I wasn't afraid to admit it.

She began to swivel her hips, searching for release. I would deny her unless it meant greater gratification. This wasn't one of those moments. Right now, I needed to feel her pussy strangle my cock, and I wouldn't accept anything else.

Chest heaving, I drove into her harder, faster, forcing my cock deep inside her tightness at a reckless pace until I was ramming her into the mattress. It couldn't be helped.

"Fuck, Dex!"

That's it, baby.

"Shit. Shit!" The words flew from her lips, followed by a guttural moan. Trish screamed as her orgasm seized her. Her knees wobbled as her thighs shook, and she fell on her stomach. Her wet, sticky pussy clenched me hard, and I didn't allow her to stay down, roughly yanking her back against me.

My cock throbbed. When her ass slammed against me, I came with a choked rasp. A shudder rolled through me as I finally began to slow, pumping a couple of times as I whispered a wish.

"Give me another baby, Trish."

She exhaled, trying to catch her breath. "Creed does need a sibling."

Hearing her say that, I grew hard again in an instant. I began to thrust, gliding in and out of her, deciding I needed to see her face and feel her tits smashed against my chest. I needed her warmth heating me up from the inside out.

Pulling out, I flipped her over, draping my body over hers as I reentered her tight channel. Heavy-lidded eyes locked on mine as I began to slowly fuck her a second time.

My mouth lowered to hers, latching with a fevered kiss. "I fucking love you, Trish."

"I'll love you until the day I die, Dex, maybe longer."

With our breaths mingling, I picked up the pace.

We didn't get much sleep after that.

ROYAL BASTARDS MC

Chapter 6

TRiSH

"I FORGOT HOW DIFFERENT it is here," Faith observed. "The pulse of life is so much faster. In Ohio, it feels slower and more relaxed. Here, everything feels rushed, like people are afraid life will pass them by if they don't hurry."

"Yeah, I can see that. It's the West Coast. Cali, Nevada, and Washington. Always a hustle."

"I don't miss it," she laughed.

No, I didn't think she did.

I sat back against the bench, where we stopped to let Jessa and Creed run off some of their excess energy. The duo climbed all over a massive jungle gym area with slides and animals. I liked coming here because of the kid-friendly sculpted foam used to create the different elements.

It was safe and always kept clean, plus the enclosed area meant my little wild child couldn't run out without me catching him since I stayed close to the only entry/exit.

"I think I would feel that way, too, if not for Grim and the club. There's consistency in their way of life that doesn't change. It's a bit crazy at times, but I love it."

"It's a good fit for you. When you first dated Grim, I worried you'd end up hurt, or he'd become violent. I'm glad I was wrong." Faith reached for my hand and squeezed it. "I'm sorry I left you to deal with our dad and Moby's shit. I know it wasn't easy."

She didn't know the details. I never told her Moby was the reason I miscarried. She knew he was to blame for our father's death, but she also knew the man who raised us was a lazy piece of shit who only cared about himself.

I gulped as I fought to swallow the sudden lump in my throat. God. Thinking of that mess dragged so much shit back up from the past—things I wanted to forget because they didn't matter now. I wouldn't let the people who hurt me have that kind of control, especially now that they were gone.

"It's okay. I get why you left. You needed to escape." I shrugged. "I should have done it sooner myself."

"Trish. I should have been there for you."

"You're here now. We don't have to let the past come back and haunt us."

"I suppose you're right. I just feel guilty," she admitted. "When you came to visit before Creed was born, I could see how traumatized you were from all the shit that happened. I really am sorry, sis."

"I know. All is forgiven. Truly." I hugged my sister, blinking back tears. Her words meant a lot to me because there was a time I would have done anything to hear them.

It was a full-circle moment. I realized just how far I had come, clawing my way back after a severe depression. I thought my life was over when I lost my baby, and things ended with Grim. They were dark days. But now, I could see how going through that experience enabled me to appreciate the present.

I'd fought to heal and find my way back to Grim. We had Creed. All the loss and sacrifice seemed worth it, although I would never wish anyone to go through what I did. It was fucking awful.

But now? I could say I was truly happy.

"You're different," Faith observed. "Stronger. At peace, too, I think."

"I am," I agreed.

We turned to the kids, watching Jessa beat Creed to an enormous turtle. He pouted, stomping his foot.

"My turtle, Jess!"

Faith sighed. "My daughter, always the one causing trouble."

I laughed as she hopped up, rushing to the kids.

My shoulders relaxed as I released a breath, finally able to say that I had reached a point in my life where I felt the ghosts of my past couldn't harm me. I felt free.

The kids continued to argue over the play toys, and I knew they'd gotten cranky because they were tired. There was only so much a two-year-old boy and three-year-old girl could handle before they lost their shit.

With a smile, I stood, trying to wrangle Creed. He shot off as I reached him, giggling as he climbed toward a slide.

My boy. The rebel. Just like his father.

I had to stifle a laugh as I moved to the bottom of the slide, ready to catch him when he slid down.

Creed waved. "Catch me, Mama!"

Always.

He pushed off and zoomed toward me as I scooped him up, peppering kisses on his cheeks, nose, and head. I knew he was tired when his head rested on my shoulder.

"My eyes are screaming," he whispered.

So cute.

Creed always said that when he was sleepy.

"We're going home for a snack and a nap, little man."

My gaze swept over the play area, looking for Faith. She was chasing Jessa and probably needed a few minutes to catch her. I returned to our stuff, buckling Creed into the stroller. I learned long ago that he was too heavy to carry long distances. Grim never had a problem with that, but he had about a hundred pounds of extra muscle to handle it.

Packed and ready, I approached the exit when I noticed a man in a dark gray hoodie. The front was pulled low enough to conceal his features, but I couldn't help cringing when I realized he was watching me. Staring, he never moved, and the stranger blocked the only retreat.

Shit.

Something about him seemed familiar. We'd met before. I recognized his stance, as odd as that sounded. He stood in a way that seemed almost threatening. Dangerous.

Although the mall was air-conditioned, no one else wore a hoodie or jacket today. The temperature had reached eighty before we left The Crossroads.

Who the hell was this guy? What did he want?

My protective instincts kicked in. No one would harm me or my family. Oddly enough, I thought of Razr. Grim said he wasn't a threat any longer because they reaped his soul.

But why did I feel like the stranger resembled Razr?

"Trish! I'm so sorry."

I turned to my sister, biting my lip to hold back laughter as she struggled with a crying preschooler. "It's okay."

Faith managed to buckle Jessa into her stroller next to mine. I lifted my head and faced the exit.

The stranger was gone. A glance around the play area proved he vanished. Weird.

"What's wrong?"

I blinked. "Nothing. We're good."

She nodded. "Let's get these little ones home. I think I need a nap, too," she joked.

"Definitely," I agreed.

ALL FOUR OF US slept for nearly three hours. The kids had tuckered out from playing. Faith needed the rest since early pregnancy wiped her out. And me? I'd had a vigorous evening between the sheets with Grim and not much rest the night before. All of us woke up refreshed.

I could smell pasta and sauce as I opened my eyes, slipping from the bed to wander into the hall. My stomach rumbled when I entered the kitchen.

Grim glanced my way with a wink. "I figured everyone would want dinner, so I made spaghetti with meat sauce and garlic bread, and I've got stuff to toss a salad."

He was so good to me. "You're the best." I popped a kiss on his cheek.

"My master plan to keep you addicted and in need."

"Oh? Is that so?" I asked, reaching around to cup his crotch as he stirred the spaghetti.

"Angel, I will fuck you on this counter right now. Don't tempt me."

"What if someone comes in?"

He flashed a devious grin. "That's the point."

I pouted, pulling my hand away. "I don't want to traumatize my sister."

"Please don't," she laughed from behind us.

Grim snorted. "Wouldn't dream of it."

"Yeah, you would," she contradicted. "I married a Marine. I know how you wild guys operate."

Grim laughed hard, shaking his head. "I suppose you're right about that."

Over the next week, I spent most of my time with my sister and niece. Her visits were rare, so I hoped no one felt neglected around The Crossroads. They would have to forgive me.

A few days before her departure, I rolled over in bed, confused when I heard whispering. My eyes snapped open when I realized the voices were coming through the monitor.

Grim lightly snored beside me, and I slid from the mattress, wondering if Jessa had joined Creed in his room. I lingered outside my son's door, listening as he giggled.

"Grrrr."

Silence.

"Ghrowl. I like it."

I shit you not; out of nowhere, I heard something respond to him. A rumbling roar followed, filling the room with a terrifying growl that sounded awfully close to a bear. It wasn't a bear, though, because the deepness of it felt different. Almost ghost-like, which didn't make sense.

My mouth opened to scream for Grim as I rushed into the room, terrified for Creed. "Baby, come here."

"Mama, it's okay." He giggled again. "I'm safe."

Safe. What did a two-year-old child know about that? Had he heard adults talking and decided to mimic the words?

I dropped to my knees beside his bed and pulled him into my embrace. My frantic gaze bounced around the room. I couldn't see anything, but that didn't mean we were alone.

"Mama?"

"Yeah, honey?"

"It's okay. Grrrr."

He growled again. I had no clue what that meant.

"Let's go to bed in Mommy and Daddy's room," I whispered, suddenly remembering every horror movie I had ever watched. No demon thing was coming after my child. I just had to get back to Grim so he could let his Reaper wake up.

"Mama." Creed sounded annoyed. My little man tugged on my shirt. "No. Safe. Grrrr. Ghrowl."

"Is everything okay?" I heard Grim's voice, groggy from sleep. He stood in the doorway, naked from the waist up. He must have thrown on a pair of loose pants when he heard us through the monitor.

"Sure." I rose to my feet and carried a wiggling Creed to the door.

Grim reached for his son, tucking him close to his side with one arm. Creed reached over and tickled his beard.

"He's sleeping with us the rest of the night."

A dark brow arched in curiosity, but Grim nodded. "Alright, little man. Sleepover time." He lifted his fist, and Creed bumped it.

The rest of the night passed without incident.

In the morning, after breakfast, Grim asked me what happened.

"Babe. Did Creed have a nightmare last night?"

"No, but I heard him talking to someone. No one was in the room, Dex."

"You're sure?"

"Yes."

"That's strange."

"Not as strange as the noise I heard." I described the sound, shivering as goose bumps rose on my arms. "It was scary but also weirdly familiar. I don't know."

"Hmm. I'll check into it. See if I can find out what's going on. Maybe the monitor is picking up someone else's conversation. It happens."

"But the growl?"

"Yeah, I don't know about that one." He narrowed his eyes. "I'll make sure it isn't Rael."

Poor Rael. If anything odd happened, he got blamed first. To be fair, he was often the culprit.

"Let me know what you find out."

He was already in church when I realized I had never mentioned the stranger outside the play area. I kept forgetting to say something, distracted by Faith's visit and my son's endless energy. Being out of routine shuffled everything into a mess. I saw less of Grim with all the activities we planned with the kids. But the more I thought about it, the more I dismissed the whole incident as paranoia.

I lived with the Grim Reaper. Nothing was going to hurt my family.

ROYAL BASTARDS MC

Chapter 7

GRiM

"WELL? SEE ANYTHING?" I asked, crossing my arms over my chest.

Rael shook his head. Mammoth sighed.

"Anyone? Any Scorpions MC members?"

"I walked through all of their compounds," Wraith informed me. "It's a ghost town. They're all abandoned."

Then that was it. They were gone.

"Fuck," I breathed out, releasing the tension in my shoulders. "Good."

We must have felt residual evil from Razr's presence, like phantom limb pain. It made sense. Time would erase the stain of the BSMC in Nevada.

I stood, picking up the gavel and banging it down. "Church is dismissed."

I had worried for over a week about Razr and his fucking club. Now, all I wanted was my ol' lady. Faith would be leaving in a few days, and soon, I'd have her all to myself again. Was it selfish? Fuck yeah. Did I care? Hell no.

I only liked to share Trish's time with my son. Well, and my Reaper. He rumbled my chest with approval. *You're welcome.*

My focus turned to my woman, and I left the chapel, striding down the hall toward the stairs with purpose. When I reached our apartment, I entered, relieved to discover Faith had taken a nap with Jessa. Pregnant women and children always seemed to need extra rest.

I found Trish in our room, rocking Creed. Sure, he was two, but the little guy loved snuggling until he fell asleep. Every night that I could, I stayed with him. The rest of the time, Trish put our son to sleep. As I entered the room, I caught the flutter of her eyes, and her chin dipped.

She caught herself, snapping awake as her gaze found me and softened. "Hi," she whispered.

My reaper fucking loved seeing her in our room, holding our son, content and happy. We would do *anything to* ensure the safety of Trish and Creed. He puffed my chest, striking a pose.

She bit her lip to hold back a laugh.

He became aroused at the sight of her, already wanting to show her how much we both desired her.

Not now, I told him. *We need to ride.*

In the beginning, I didn't speak to my Reaper as I do now. Our bond, like most of my brothers in the Tonopah chapter of the Royal Bastards MC, had found the symbiotic relationship challenging. Reapers had tempers and often tried to exert their will over ours. We shared a form of mutualism with a dose of competition, a healthy bit of conflict, and a respect formed with both entities.

To some, it would seem strange. Horrifying, even.

But the demonic beings that formed a shared consciousness and provided protection for our frail human bodies also enabled us to keep the club and the people we cared about safe. Our enemies had grown bolder over time. The Reapers enjoyed the thought of slaughter, specifically the first grim. *Me.* At least, the first that Lucifer signed into a contract other than ordering to reap at his will.

I still didn't understand Lucifer's reasoning, but it didn't matter. He loved to be in control. The devil got off on secrets, games, and his contracts more than a fist around his cock. The sick fucker usually pissed us off when he decided to show his face, so my loyalty remained to the members of my club, my woman, my child, and that was fucking it.

She's beautiful.

My Reaper refocused my attention. *She's stunning.*

And ours.

No debate from me.

Trish's thick cascade of platinum hair tumbled over her shoulders in waves of gold. Stopping just above her waist, the long strands curled and beckoned my fingers to dive into the silky texture. She had a full-lipped and seductive smile. Pretty blue eyes so electric they flashed through me like bolts of lightning. A rockin' body with curves.

My goddess.

But her aura I loved the most. It pulsed brighter as she slowly rose to her feet and placed Creed in bed. He remained asleep as she covered him and backed away from the bed.

Her soft hand closed around mine. "We made such a wonderful baby."

We did. That was one of the reasons I wanted more.

"He's perfect." I tugged her toward the door. "Come on."

"Where are we going?"

"Cruisin'," I answered with a husky whisper.

It seemed like forever since I had my woman on the back of my bike. It wasn't safe until I dealt with Razr and reaped the last of our enemies. Now, I didn't have any barrier to ridin' with Trish out in the open.

We stopped by our room so Trish could change clothes first. Ten minutes later, I had my ol' lady behind me as we glided from the parking lot on my Harley. Her thighs pressed to mine while her hands wrapped around my waist. Tits and pussy right up against me. If I had a preferred way to spend time with her other than fucking, this was it.

The wind whipped through my hair and billowed across our clothes. I insisted she wear a helmet, but I could tell she felt the same exhilaration I did. Her hands squeezed my stomach.

We rode for over an hour, and it couldn't have been more perfect outdoors—cloudless blue sky. Bright sunshine. A slight crisp to the wind but enough heat to prevent growing cold.

A grin widened my lips as I realized we had all the time in the world to ride and go cruisin' as often as we wanted. Freedom was a beautiful thing. Knees in the breeze. A little blacktop heaven.

Nothing sweeter.

I COULDN'T REMEMBER THE last time I took a ride anywhere alone. As the president of a motorcycle club, I always had a shadow. If I checked my mirrors, Rael or Mammoth usually followed me. If not them, one of the other officers.

So when I had a chance to ride off the lot and let the wind blow through my hair without worrying about retaliation from the Scorpions MC or Razr, I took it. Felt fucking good too. No worries. No war. No threat to Trish or Creed or anyone else that I cared about.

I took the time to ride to Las Vegas and the auto shop where I bought my parts when I worked on one of my custom bikes. That work had also taken a back seat to the shit with Razr and BSMC. I missed working with my hands and getting dirty, creating unique designs that customers loved. That was why I began Reaper's Custom Rides & Repairs.

Pulling up to the shop, I parked in front of the store, kicking down the stand after I cut the engine. Stashing my helmet inside my saddlebags, I turned the lock and walked inside.

There was something about the smell and the atmosphere in a garage or auto shop. Grease. Motor oil. Leather. Smoke. Often musty and almost always stinking like chemicals, it could sting your nose. I fucking loved it.

Stan moved from behind the counter as I approached. "Dex Lanford. Where the hell have you been, man?"

"Busy," I replied with a laugh. "I came to check on some parts I ordered last week. I was hopin' they were in."

He nodded, gesturing to his computer. "Let me look up your account."

I waited as he typed on the keyboard.

"That's strange."

"What?" I asked, wondering if the order was delayed.

"All your orders are canceled. Even the repeat orders scheduled for each month. Your account is suspended."

The fuck?

"I've never had that happen before."

"Yeah. It's weird. Looks like someone called in and asked to have the whole account blocked."

"I sure as fuck didn't."

He pointed to the screen. "Would anyone from your shop have a reason to do it?"

Fuck no. "No, Stan. We need those parts. Nobody would sabotage the company."

He nodded. I heard him clicking on the keys. "I've got it reinstated, but I'm going to have to reorder all your parts and products. It's going to take weeks to get it all in stock."

"Don't you keep some of those items on hand?"

"Yeah, but we're sold out. Every part you ordered is on backorder. Never seen anything like it. Almost like someone is trying to cut you out of the equation or impact your sales."

Yeah. It sure sounded like it. Who the fuck had a vendetta against me or the club?

I had to look into this.

"Thanks, Stan. I'm going to head back to The Crossroads. Let me know when you have the shit I need."

"Sorry, man. I'll do what I can."

"I know. Not your fault. I appreciate it."

Spinning on my heel, I walked back out, pulling on my shades as I sat on my bike. Something was going on. There was no way all of that was a coincidence.

Maybe this had to do with the reason my Reaper felt antsy.

When I returned to the compound, I found Xenon immediately, stopping to explain what had happened.

"Damn, pres. That's some vile shit."

"I need to know what you can find. Dig deep. If we've got a rival or someone looking to harm the club, I need to know."

"You got it, pres."

ROYAL BASTARDS MC

Chapter 8

TRiSH

"M<small>AMA.</small>"

C<small>REED CRAWLED ONTO</small> the couch between me and Grim, resting his head on my lap.

"What is it, baby?"

"I'm hot."

My hand moved to his forehead, finding it warm. Too warm.

He had a fever.

"Aw, does anything hurt?"

"My mouth." He opened it and pointed to his back teeth.

Grim reached for Creed. "Let me see, son." After he looked inside, Grim frowned. "Looks like some swollen nubs in there."

Creed's eyes widened. "What are nubs?"

"Well, when you're a big, strong, growing boy, your teeth get bigger too. They grow in, and sometimes it hurts a little," Grim explained.

"I don't like it."

Grim's lips twitched. "I don't like to hurt either." He ruffled Creed's hair. "Why don't we give you some Tylenol chewies, and you snuggle with Daddy? We can watch Cars."

Creed loved the Cars movies, anything with cars, trucks, or motorcycles. Like his father, he was a gearhead.

After setting up my guys with snacks, drinks, and a blanket, I brought Creed Tylenol chewies. He loved the grape flavor. I planned to check in with the pediatrician, but I guessed Creed's two-year molars were coming in. He kept sniffling, too, another sign that confirmed it. He always had a clear run when he was teething as a baby.

Grim had stretched out on our sofa. The big, inked biker barely fit across it but shared the space with our son. Creed snuggled beside him, propping Cuddles on Grim's chest. Adorable.

I checked in with my sister, pausing in the doorway of the guest room. "Are you all packed?" I asked Faith. "Need any help?"

"Nope. This is the last of it."

"I can't believe you're leaving already. This visit went by way too fast."

"I know." She shut her suitcase and zipped it up. "I'll try to come back sooner. We shouldn't go half a year before we see one another."

"I agree."

I helped her bring all the luggage into the living room. We set it by the door, finalizing the last of the details before we drove to the airport.

She needed to leave soon, as her flight departed in two hours.

I turned to the couch, intending to tell Grim I'd be gone for a few hours, when I found him asleep. Creed clutched his bear to his chest, eyes closed. They looked so precious I had to get a picture. I pulled my phone out of my pocket and snapped a few photos.

Grim had become a wonderful, loving father to his son. I thought I couldn't love him more until I saw how he cared for his child, was patient and understanding, and taught him about life with skills I could never imitate.

"Auntie Trish?"

I blinked, turning to Jessa. "Yeah, honey?"

"I'm going to miss you and Creed."

"What about Uncle Dex?" Faith asked.

"He's growly."

Yeah, Grim could be intimidating without realizing it.

"Jessa," Faith warned.

"What, Mommy? You said always tell the truth."

I snickered. "Yes, telling the truth is important."

"See?"

Faith sighed. "She's a handful."

No doubt about it. My sister could handle her daughter and the new baby. She was a great mother.

"Well, we should get going."

Faith nodded. "Let's go, Jessa."

Grim and Creed rested as I locked the door. On my way downstairs, I spotted Shadow and Zane, who helped us carry out the luggage and pack one of the SUVs.

It wasn't long before we arrived at the airport and parked, checking in at the terminal to print tickets. I walked Faith and Jessa to the gate, already trying not to cry.

"Hey," she whispered when she turned to me. "Don't start that. With my hormones, I'll be bawling the entire plane ride."

"I know," I sniffled. "Give me a hug."

She held on for longer than I would have thought before we separated. Jessa threw her little arms around my legs.

"Auntie Trish, bear hug."

I picked her up, wrapping her in my embrace as I squeezed. "Is that good?"

"Yes!"

I set her back down, smiling as she reached for Faith's hand. "Let me know when you arrive home safe so I don't worry."

"I will. Love you, sis."

"Love ya back."

As soon as I turned away from my sister, I fought tears. They stung my eyes, and I blinked rapidly, lifting my chin as I walked through the airport. I probably should have been aware of my surroundings, but I wasn't. I hated goodbyes.

When I reached the SUV, I clicked the fob and opened the driver's side door. I sat down, tossed my purse on the passenger side, and closed the door. Out of habit, I hit the lock button and glanced in the mirror. Dashing under my eyes, I removed the few tears that had fallen.

I had the weirdest feeling as I reached for my seatbelt and draped it across my chest. My skin prickled with awareness. It was strange. I clicked the belt into place and started the engine, lifting my head to scan the parking garage.

When I initially arrived, I backed in so it would be easier to unload all the luggage. Facing the lane in front of me and another row of cars, I found a stranger leaning against a black truck. It wasn't the vehicle that worried me.

The man stood still, staring at me through the windshield. He wore the same hoodie as the man from the play area where I brought Faith and Jessa last week.

In fact, I would bet it was the same person.

Shit.

He didn't move. Like our previous encounter, he never spoke or tried to contact me. He just *stared*.

Now, I was creeped out.

Whatever this man wanted, I didn't care to find out. I pushed on the gas and sped out of the lot, taking the turns a little too fast. Luckily, I didn't run into much traffic. I breathed a sigh of relief when I left the stranger far behind.

One of my favorite songs popped up on the radio, and I turned up the volume, rocking out as I drove. About twenty minutes outside of Tonopah, I felt the car jolt. My gaze flicked to the rearview mirror. Behind me, the black truck revved its engine, gunning toward me a second time.

Fuck!

I pressed down on the gas pedal, picking up speed. This lunatic was trying to kill me!

With a shaky finger, I pushed the phone symbol on the steering wheel. "Call Dex."

"Calling Dex," the robotic, husky female voice replied.

The line rang five times before Grim answered. "Babe?"

"Someone is following me from the airport."

"What?"

"A guy is wearing a hoodie, and I can't see his face. He's driving a black truck. Grim, he hit the back bumper once already."

"Fuck, babe. Stay calm. Where are you?"

"Too far out," I screamed as the guy hit me again, a little harder than last time. "Dex!"

"Trish, hold on, baby. I'm riding out right now!"

"What about Creed?"

Yeah, I needed to know my son was safe at that moment.

"He's good. Sasha is with him."

Sasha. Thank fuck.

Flashing lights appeared as the high beams switched on behind me, glaring through the rearview mirror. It hurt my eyes as I tried to focus on the road.

"Where are you, Trish?"

The rumble of motorcycles came through the line.

"About five miles out."

"We're on our way. You keep drivin', baby. Hear me? You'll see me real soon."

"Okay." The tremor in my voice betrayed my anxiety.

Glancing at the truck, I noticed he had slowed down. The vehicle became smaller in the mirror as the distance between us grew. Before long, I could only see a black spec that disappeared into the desert.

Shaken, I bit my lip, trying to remain in control.

I saw Grim's bike along with a half dozen other Royal Bastards. They rode fast toward me as I pressed on the brake, skidding to a halt on the side of the road.

Grim swung his bike toward me, gravel flying behind his tire as he finally stopped. I watched him lift off the seat and run toward me, flinging open the door.

I was in his arms, trembling, as he smoothed my hair, trying to calm me. "Babe." I leaned back, staring into the face of the Reaper. With a jolt, I blinked.

"Not tryin' to scare you."

"I know."

"Worried. Pissed." The words left his lips with an inhuman growl.

This version of Dex, the man I loved, was more Grim Reaper than biker.

"I'm scared."

"Not anymore. I'm here. You're safe."

"Okay."

"Babe, we need to talk. I don't know what's happening, but you can't go anywhere alone. Not until I figure this out. Okay? Promise me."

His Reaper had receded once he knew I was physically unharmed. I stared into the handsome face of my biker boyfriend. Well, my old man. My rider or die. Truly, other than Creed, he was my everything.

"I promise."

ROYAL BASTARDS MC

Chapter 9

GRiM

"I NEED TO KNOW who the fuck this was, Xenon. Everything about this motherfucker. He's after my woman."

"I know, pres."

"He fucking hit her bumper. He almost wrecked her."

"I hear you. I'm on it. We'll fucking get him, pres. He can't hide for long."

This shit was so fucked. As soon as she was safe, someone fucked with her. Un*fucking*acceptable.

"You want me to keep digging about bike parts too?"

"Yeah." I started to walk away when I spun on my heel. "Maybe they're connected. I don't like surprises. Don't leave me in the fucking dark, Xenon. You're the only one who can figure this shit out."

"I'll have answers for you soon," he swore.

Yeah, not soon enough.

I returned to Trish, slipping into our apartment since I wasn't sure if my family was awake yet. Both Trish and Creed had gone to bed, and I left them resting peacefully together on our bed while I checked in with Xenon. Other than that, I wasn't doing anything else. My woman and my son needed me. Everyone else could fuck off.

I poked my head into the room, noting that Trish's eyes were open. "Hey."

She untangled herself from Creed and slid off the mattress, covering him with a blanket before walking my way. We closed the door to a crack, allowing us to hear when he woke up.

"I've seen that man once before," she began. "I'm sorry I forgot to mention it. At the time, I thought it wasn't a big deal, that maybe I was being paranoid."

"What happened?" I asked, fixing her a cup of hot tea. I ran Earl Gray through the Keurig and set the mug in front of her, reaching into the fridge to set the sliced lemons on the counter.

She smiled as she reached for the honey and added a lemon slice. "He came to the play place the day I took Faith and the kids. They were so tired when we left. Faith had to chase Jessa to get her into the stroller. It was kinda chaotic."

"I bet."

"I buckled Creed in when I noticed the stranger watching me. It gave me a weird vibe, but I got distracted when my sister joined me. I looked back, and he was gone."

"That's bizarre," I agreed. "What did he look like?"

"That's just it. I couldn't say. Average build. Broad shoulders. Maybe six feet tall. He wore a gray hoodie that disguised his features. I didn't see his face. He wore gloves, too."

Fuck. This sounded like a pro. He gave her nothing to go on— no distinguishing marks or characteristics. No tattoos. She didn't know his hair or eye color or even his nationality.

Who the fuck had a vendetta against me?

My Reaper was growing fucking pissed. He almost lost his shit when we rolled up to the SUV and saw her shaking, gripping the steering wheel because she was so fucking scared.

When I found this asshole, he was going to fucking suffer for this. No fast reaping for him. I would drag it out until he screamed and begged for death.

But the worst part of all this was finally settling into a normal life. I didn't want our entire relationship to be tainted by my life in the club, never able to go out and do the shit ordinary people did. We never had many dates. Couldn't go to the movies or a fancy dinner. Razr and the Scorpions MC had made it impossible with our feud.

I promised her I would change that. I swore to make it up to her. And I didn't want this sick fuck to mess this up.

No, I wouldn't let him. I would take Trish out and do the shit I promised. Fuck this asshole. I'd have some of the members follow us and create a perimeter. We'd be safe. Trish would get that sweet, perfect night she always wanted with me. I couldn't let her down.

"Babe."

"Dex?"

"You remember that date you wanted to go on?"

"Yes." She frowned. "It's a weird time to bring that up."

"Maybe, but I won't let this bastard get away with trying to spook us. Xenon is looking into it. We'll find him on camera and his truck. This guy won't be in the wind for long."

"Grim."

She always called me that when she was trying to reason with the overprotective and stubborn part of my personality.

"I want to take you out. Sasha won't mind staying with Creed. He's fine. Fever broke this afternoon. He's been playing with his toys and talking to Cuddles."

She smiled at that. "Seems dangerous. I can't believe I'm the one saying this instead of you."

My Reaper growled. He fucking agreed.

"I know. But I'll be with you. You'll never be alone. We won't be riding out without backup."

She tilted her head, considering my words. "I don't know."

It took some convincing, but I finally got her to agree to our date.

"Look, Trish, we have to live our life, right? There's always going to be an element of danger. We can't let it stop us from enjoying what we want to do and having those dates you've always wanted."

I had her now. I could see it.

"Okay."

I didn't tell her the other reason I wanted to take her out in public. I was hoping I could draw out this cowardly fuck who kept messing with Trish without revealing his identity. If this cocksucker saw us together and thought he could get to her, then he'd try to make a move. When he did, a dozen Reapers would be there to harvest his soul.

I wasn't going to be intimidated by the cocksucker. He wanted to play, we'd fucking play. But I was a master at this game after twenty years, and he would find out fast that he had messed with the wrong club.

Four hours later, I rode out of Tonopah and toward Pahrump. There was a steak house known for some of the best beef in the state. I figured the warm weather and beautiful ride would relax her before we got our fill of steak and shared a big slice of chocolate cake. My ol' lady was gonna get treated like a queen tonight. She deserved it.

Club members followed us at a distance. Not everyone rode a bike. Rael insisted on his Harley. So did Mammoth. Bodie drove one of the SUVs with Shadow. Several other members took cars that wouldn't be recognized or affiliated with our businesses. None of the guys wore their cuts, either. I hated to order them to leave them behind, but they were on recon and guard duty all night. We didn't want this stalker to know how many club members had followed Trish and me.

I held the door open for Trish once we reached the steak house and parked the bike. She entered before me, and I took a moment to appreciate her juicy ass. Fuck. I couldn't wait to get her back home later and grab her hips, pulling her into my face as I stuck my tongue in her pussy.

But that was my dessert. She'd get hers first.

Since I made a reservation, we were seated right away, tucked into the back, where I could see every entrance and exit without appearing too obvious. I didn't trust this fucker not to try to catch us by surprise.

My phone pinged with a text. I took it from my cut and checked the screen.

"Everything okay?"

"Perfect. Everyone is in place."

"That sounds ominous," she joked.

"Babe. I'm taking every precaution. Relax. Enjoy the meal. I want this to be fun for you."

She smiled, reaching over the table to hold my hand. "I know. I appreciate it."

We almost had to waddle out of the restaurant an hour and a half later. I swear to fuck; we ordered enough food to feed fifty people. Trish got that chocolate dessert she wanted, and I had my Kobe steak.

I held the door open for Trish and let her through, balancing the containers of leftovers. We definitely had lunch tomorrow.

I led her to my bike, walking toward it when I saw something sticking out of the seat. On closer inspection, I realized there was a fucking knife shoved through the leather, and a single photograph had been stabbed through the center.

Trish.

A photo of her holding my son at the play area the same day she told me she'd gone with Faith and Jessa.

My woman wasn't paranoid. Someone was targeting her. And I didn't know who, why, or how they fuck they got to my bike.

A roar left my chest as my Reaper surfaced. I dropped the bags of food, pulling her into my chest. My gaze flicked over the entire vicinity as I scanned for threats. We were alone.

My Reaper sensed nothing. No familiar scents. No strange or dark auras. Nothing that would alert me to danger.

I wrapped my arm around Trish and held her against me as I called Xenon. "Someone just stabbed a knife through my fucking seat."

"Shit," he cursed. "You at the restaurant?"

Xenon knew the plan for this evening. I told him to be alert in case that fucker showed up.

"Tap into cameras and find who the fuck did this. I want to know. Drop what you're doing and find them. Fucking now!"

I hung up without waiting for a reply.

Bodie and Shadow pulled up in the SUV. "Need a ride, pres?"

"Yes," I growled, opening the door and helping Trish inside.

"Grim?"

"Yeah, baby?" I asked as I joined her.

"I want my chocolate cake." She sniffled, and I realized she had been crying.

Fuck!

"Yeah, I'll get it."

"No, I will, pres."

Shadow jumped out as I shut the door. He grabbed the bags for us and set them on the front seat. "I'll ride your bike back."

"Thanks." I slapped my keys into his palm. "Try not to rip her any further."

"I'll be gentle." He winked and walked to my Harley, firing it up before following us as Bodie drove back toward Tonopah.

I held Trish against me, fighting every instinct to go hunt this fucker down. She needed me more than I needed his suffering. But that would only last as long as it took to calm her.

The problem was that I still didn't know how the fuck was messing with her. Now, I knew it wasn't just about Trish. She was a way to get to me, and this sick fucker knew my weakness.

It still didn't change the most disturbing news of all.

How the fuck did this guy elude our Reapers?

ROYAL BASTARDS MC

Chapter 10

GRiM

"I DON'T GET HOW this fucker got to your bike without any of us seeing him," Mammoth snarled the following morning in church.

"We were watching, pres," Rael promised.

"I know. That's what fucking worries me."

"But the area was fucking crowded. He managed to blend in. No other explanation, pres."

I nodded to Shadow. "Maybe."

"Or he knew we would recognize him, so he used a decoy," Wraith guessed.

"Fuck," I spat, shoving away from the table as I began to pace. "I bet you're right. There weren't any recognizable scents or auras. No one stood out. Whoever this asshole is, he knows what he's doing."

"Which means he won't stop, pres," Mammoth concluded.

"No. He won't." I punched at the nearest wall, unable to control my temper. "He's not just after Trish. He stabbed a knife through a photo of my family. Creed is a target, too."

Rage flashed through my body like molten fire. This motherfucker had no idea that he just fucked with the Grim Reaper. Death was my fucking playground.

"What are you thinkin', pres?" Bodie asked, cracking his neck. "Want to send us on a hunting spree?"

"No. He's going to come to us. I can sense it. Trish and Creed are on lockdown. They remain at The Crossroads until this threat is eliminated."

Heads nodded as my brothers agreed.

Xenon opened the door to the chapel and walked in. "Got news for you, pres."

"Tell me."

"I looked into all those cameras, and the feeds from last night caught a teenager with spiky black hair and saggy jeans stabbing the knife through the seat. He took off after he did it. Looked nervous the whole time, like he was scared he'd get caught."

"You track him down?"

"I didn't have to," he sighed.

"Why?" I wasn't going to like his answer. I could feel it.

"He's one of Zane's best friends."

Wraith shot to his feet. "The fuck? Xenon, if you're fucking around, I swear to fuck, I'll kick your ass."

He snorted. "I'm not Rael."

Rael lifted a middle finger in his direction.

"Here. See for yourself." Xenon flipped around the laptop he brought with him. "See? Here's the feed from last night." He hit a couple of keys. "And here's Zane last week with Sid."

The same fucking kid. Sid Connor.

I met him once. What the fuck was this about?

"Wraith, get Zane in here now."

"You got it, pres." He marched to the door of the chapel and hollered for his son. Zane and Wraith were close. I could see the torment in his expression. He didn't like this any more than I did.

I didn't believe for a second that Zane would betray the club. But his friend? Didn't trust him at all. Hell, I didn't know the kid.

Zane entered through the chapel as Wraith shut the door. He turned to his father, blinked, then glanced at me. "Pres?"

"I need you to look at something."

Zane nodded.

"Show him, Xenon."

The video feed from last night played. When Xenon paused on Sid's face as he stabbed the knife through my fucking bike seat, Zane paled.

"Shit." He swallowed. Hard. "Dad, I don't know what this is about. I fucking swear." He took a couple of steps in my direction. "I would never betray the club."

"I believe you, but your friend isn't loyal to us. He's not a Royal Bastard or a prospect."

"He's not a bad guy. There's just some shit going on at home," Zane began, then stopped. "No excuses. What do you want me to do?"

"Ask him to meet you. Tell him you need to talk or whatever the fuck you have to say to convince him to show up."

"Okay, pres." Zane pulled his phone from the front pocket of his jeans and sent off a few texts.

It didn't take long to receive a reply.

"He can meet me in an hour."

"Rael, Wraith, and Shadow go with Zane. Bring back Sid."

"If he tries to run?"

"Use force," I growled. "He knows the identity of the guy scaring Trish and going after my son. I don't care how he arrives. Get him here."

"I'll make sure he's with us," Wraith promised.

"I'm holding you to it."

After I dismissed church, I needed to clear my head. My Reaper wanted to unleash a bloody hunting spree across the city, and I had cut him off, refusing to allow his dark thoughts to consume me.

I went upstairs, anxious to check on Trish and Creed.

"Hey," I greeted her as I entered the living room, dropping beside her on the couch.

"Hi," Trish replied before lowering her head to rest her cheek on my shoulder.

I slid an arm around her and tugged her closer into my body.

Creed played on the floor in front of us, zooming his Tonka vehicles and the plastic motorcycle I bought him for his last birthday across the rug. It was one of those designs with roads, streetlights, stop signs, and even a few buildings and trees. Creed loved it.

"Hi, Daddy."

"Hi, little man."

Creed giggled. "Grrrr."

"I still don't know why he does that."

"Me either," I confessed, "but it's adorable."

"Grrrr. Ghrowl. GG." Creed pointed at me. "GG, Daddy."

Gigi? What did he mean?

"I'm sorry, buddy. I don't think I know who GG is."

Creed threw one of his trucks. "Daddy. G. G."

He looked frustrated.

"Hey, no throwing toys, Creed," I growled.

He jumped up and laughed. "Daddy! Grrrr. Ghrowl!"

He seemed so excited that I pretended to understand. "Yes. Ghrowl. Grrrr."

Creed jumped onto my lap. "Wuv you."

Aw, man. I loved this kid more than I ever thought it was possible to love another person. The love for a child was indescribable.

"I love you, too. You're my special little man."

Trish lifted her head to kiss my cheek. "You're so good at this."

"That's why I want more," I teased.

"Me too."

My heart swelled with happiness. For an hour, I held my little family, fucking lucky to have them in my life.

"WHY DID YOU SHOVE a fucking knife in my bike?" I asked, standing in front of Sid.

Wraith stood beside me, arms crossed over his chest. "Tell him."

Zane rested a hand on Sid's shoulder. "Don't lie. Trust me."

"They don't know me," Sid spat. "Why would they care what I have to say?"

Zane shook his head. "You can't push everyone in your life away. We're not all looking to hurt and betray you."

"Fucking Zane. Always trying to talk me through shit like a goddamn therapist."

This kid sure had a chip on his shoulder and enough baggage to fill a cargo hold. "You gonna answer me or face the consequences?"

I wasn't going to hurt him, but I did want him to work off the damage to my bike for the cost of the repair. He wouldn't learn shit about life if someone didn't try to set him straight.

Sid scoffed. "I'm a minor. You can't touch me."

I let a little of the Reaper surface, enough to convince him I didn't give a shit about the fact he hadn't turned eighteen yet. "Wanna bet?"

Something in my tone or expression must have spooked him. "Shit."

"Speak up," Wraith ordered.

"I, uh, got paid to do it."

Paid. Just like we guessed. "You see the guy?"

"No. He wore a gray hoodie. Gloves. Sunglasses. I don't know who the fuck it was, but he paid me five hundred bucks to stab the seat with the picture."

"Do you know the woman and child in the photo?" Zane asked.

Sid shook his head.

"That's my ol' lady and my son," I thundered.

Sid backed up a couple of feet. "Oh, fuck."

"You didn't think that through, did you?" Wraith moved toward Sid, slamming his fist into the wall above his head as Sid backed against it. "Why did you do it?"

"For my sister. She's sick."

Wraith sighed.

Zane moved in front of Sid, forcing his father to back off. "It's true. Sid's little sister needs medication, and it's expensive. Their insurance sucks. It doesn't cover shit."

Fuck. I couldn't even be mad at Sid after I heard that. Yeah, I fucking hated Raptor's bike got fucked up, but now that I knew why, it fizzled my anger.

My worry switched to the man causing so much chaos in my life. Where the fuck did he come from?

"You're sure you didn't recognize the guy in the hoodie? His voice? Anything?"

"No, man. I swear."

My Reaper sensed he told the truth.

"This is what's gonna happen. "You're working for me until you've paid off the cost of my bike's repairs."

Sid swallowed. "Okay."

"You'll show up every fucking morning at nine a.m., and you won't leave until you finish the day's work. Something comes up with your family, you fucking let me know. None of this shit where I have to hunt you down again. You feel me?"

"Yeah."

"You start next Monday. Tell anyone about this shit, and I will take the video of your vandalism and share it all over social media. The police will have copies. But if you pay off your debt, we're even. Yeah?"

"Yeah. Okay, Mr."

"It's Mr. Lanford to you. Only my club members call me Pres. Only my friends call me Grim. You ain't either of those yet."

He smiled at my use of the word yet. "Okay, Mr. Lanford."

"Get out of here."

Zane flashed me a grin. "Can I go with him?"

I ticked my chin toward the door. "Go."

Once Wraith and I stood alone, he chuckled.

"You're a softie."

"Kid seems like he could use a break. Everyone must have given him shit his whole life. He's got no skills to survive."

"True. Zane cares about Sid. They're close. I appreciate it, pres."

I opened my mouth to reply when Xenon nearly crashed through the chapel doors. "Fuck, pres. You're never gonna believe this."

"What?"

"Just fucking look. You'd think I was lying if I told you. Hell, I don't want to believe my own eyes."

He pressed play, and I watched a video feed of the man in the gray hoodie. He stood in the same parking garage where she had dropped off her sister at the airport. I saw him turn to the cameras, shove his hoodie back, and smile.

He didn't have to say a word. The threat was clear without any communication. As soon as he revealed his identity, I knew I had gotten shit wrong. Somehow, I had been deceived. The entire club. Every single Reaper. We'd been played for fools.

My lip curled into a snarl. "Razr."

Xenon shook his head. "He's alive. I don't know how, pres. It doesn't make sense."

"No, it doesn't. That's the point. He wants me to know he's been fucking with me all along. Messing with Trish. The photo and the knife. Almost closing my account at the parts store."

"Fuck. I hate that asshole."

"Oh, don't worry. Now that I know, he won't be breathing for much longer."

ROYAL BASTARDS MC

Chapter 11

TRiSH

"YOU CAN'T LEAVE. GRIM said you're on lockdown."

"Well, I can't get ahold of him. I have to pick up Creed's prescription. The pediatrician says he's got an ear infection."

After all the mess with Creed's runny nose and molars coming in, he started pulling on his ears and complaining about the right one hurting. I did a telehealth visit, and the doctor said he needed an antibiotic. He called it in a few hours ago, and now I had to pick it up.

"Sorry, Trish. No can do. Grim would kick my ass."

"I'll kick your ass if you don't move out of my way, Rael."

The threat was minimal. We both knew it.

He smirked. "Trish. I'll go pick it up. Whatever you need. Just make a list."

"Do you know which diapers he needs? Which sensitive wipes for his bottom so he doesn't get a rash?"

"No. That's why you'll write it down."

"Do you know which lube to pick up for me and Grim?"

He gagged. "Jesus. Fucking. Christ."

"See? I need to go the pharmacy, Rael."

He scrubbed a hand down his face. "I swear to fuck; if you don't stay with me every second we're in there, I will chain you to my side. Grim won't care. Neither will Nylah. She likes the chains." He added that last part with a grin.

I rolled my eyes. "Text him so he knows."

Rael tried to call first. He shot off a couple of texts promising to keep me safe and that Grim could blame me for lube and shit. He showed me what he wrote. What a comedian.

I tried to ignore him as we left The Crossroads and drove fifteen minutes away to the pharmacy. He didn't care; he just kept talking about Nylah and the boys. It was cute, but I didn't tell him that. Rael had an ego the size of Texas.

"Listen," he began as we parked, "I'm following you down every aisle. Every step you take, I'm right fucking there. Anyone looks at you, I'm gonna be there to fuck them up."

"You're so weird," I sighed. "Come on."

Rael stayed annoyingly close to me in the store. He even bumped into me a few times. Ridiculous.

"I appreciate the effort, but this is starting to irritate me."

Rael shrugged. "Pres wouldn't want it any other way."

His eyes lit up, and I could see the freak the guys in the club often referred to. Rael was a little unhinged.

It was his sweet, protective side Nylah loved. And Rael took his position as SAA of the club seriously, ensuring every member and their families were always safe.

It was exhausting, but he seemed to handle it well. Maybe that was the crazy in him.

He had energy I could only dream about.

"Since you're there, be useful."

I shoved all of my shopping items into his arms.

"Trish," he warned. "I can't have my hands full like this."

"Then grab a basket," I answered sweetly.

He made a show of being put out, grabbing one of the baskets, and standing at my side.

"I just have to pick up the script, and we can leave."

"Thank fuck."

I had Creed's prescription and the bags in my hand when I turned and faced the door, catching the mirror on the wall to my right, closest to the exit. Tingling broke out on the back of my neck. And that was when I saw him.

I will never forget what he looked like after our odd meeting. It wasn't until after he left that I realized how dangerous the situation had become. Nobody at the party figured it out until it was too late.

Tilting my head to the side, I sized the guy up, wondering who he was and why he approached me without Grim. He was average as far as appearance went. He had short dark hair, a medium build, a little scruff on his face, and plain brown eyes. He wasn't handsome, and he wasn't ugly— someone who just blended into the crowd.

There was something odd about this guy and his demeanor. He must have been a friend of someone I didn't know because I'd never seen him before, and we had plenty of these gatherings in recent weeks. The bikers didn't attend before today because it was usually just the employees from the Blacktop.

"You two close?"

He didn't answer my question, instead asking another of his own, gazing into my eyes with a twisted smile that made my gut clench in warning. His voice dropped low and held an edge I wasn't comfortable around. I scooted over on the bench, farther away from where he was seated, and he narrowed his eyes, contemplating the movement.

"Smart. Not safe to talk to strangers, right?" There was a brief chuckle that lacked humor, and then he shrugged. "No worries, darlin'. You're not the fish I want to catch."

"I should find my friends."

"Yes, you should." He slowly stood and rolled his shoulders, cracking his neck as he ticked his head in my direction. "I'll be seeing you around, honey."

Feeling bold, I swallowed hard and didn't move, standing my ground even when I fought the urge to flee. "What name should I tell Grim?"

Neither of us was a fool. This guy had a vendetta or wanted to cause trouble. Maybe he was playing his own demented game.

"Razr."

He could have killed me. Grim only left me alone for a few minutes. Members of the Royal Bastards were present at that party. I should have been protected. I was supposed to be protected . . .but I wasn't. Razr took advantage of a vulnerable moment. I never forgot what he looked like or the sound of his scratchy voice.

"Rael?"

"Yeah?"

"You have your gun, right?"

He stiffened beside me. "Yeah. Why?"

"Look up at the mirror."

These pharmacy stores were all similar, with huge round mirrors in the corners that reflected whole sections of the store. A theft deterrent. They revealed sneaky hands and suspicious individuals.

Right now? The mirror revealed Grim's greatest enemy.

"Oh, fuck."

Razr was here.

"I need you to listen to me real close, Trish."

"Okay," I whispered, like it mattered.

"You're gonna move toward the door. I'll be right behind you. If he makes a move toward us, I'm pulling my gun."

"Rael, you can't do that in the store."

"The hell I can't."

Oh my God! We were going to end up on the evening news. Shot dead at a local pharmacy. Or portrayed as murdering druggies on a wild rampage. I could see the headlines.

"Trish, get out of your head. Stay alert. Get to the SUV."

Right. Focus.

I nodded as we moved toward the exit. Razr watched us with the same calculating grin until we passed him, then began to follow us.

Rael shoved the keys into my hand. "Run."

Shit!

I bolted for the SUV, yanking on the handle of the driver's side door and climbing inside. I slammed it shut, breathing hard as I turned my head to see where Rael went.

He stood in front of my window. "Razr."

"Give Grim a message."

"I'm not your errand boy, you fucking dick."

Razr took a step toward us, and Rael cracked his neck. "Give me a fucking reason. They won't find your body."

Razr ticked his chin toward the SUV. "Tell him I can get to her whenever I want. If I wanted his little bitch dead, I would have done it already."

"She's the ol' lady of my pres, motherfucker. Show some respect."

Razr shrugged. "That means nothing to me."

"How the fuck are you still alive?"

"You still haven't figured it out?" A sinister laugh followed. "I had a twin. An *identical* twin."

Rael slammed a fist into the door panel. "Fuck."

"Yeah, now I got another reason to have your fucking president. Tell him I'm done with this shit. I'll be seeing him real soon." Razr's gaze focused on me. "You change your mind and want a real man; I'm willing to put you to work on your knees, Trish."

I jolted from his crude innuendo.

Rael growled, pushing off the SUV to charge at Razr. I figured he might use his Reaper ability, but he didn't. Razr backed up a few paces until a silver van pulled up. He hopped inside, flipping the middle finger as the driver raced out of the lot.

"Always a fucking coward," Rael complained. He frowned as he turned to me. "You wanna drive or me?"

I pointed at him. I was so shaky I couldn't hold the wheel.

"Move over."

I hit the unlock button and moved seats, climbing onto the passenger side as I pushed the bags onto the floor. My nerves were shot. Anxious energy flowed through me. I chewed on a nail, staring out the window as Rael began bitching.

"I told you to fucking stay put. Said we couldn't leave. Oh no, you had to go for fucking lube."

"Rael."

"Fuck no. I'm not hearing it. You could have been hurt."

"You have your Reaper. He would have protected me."

"Not the fucking point."

"Why are you so cranky? Nothing happened."

"Fucking women, man. Do you argue about everything?"

I glared in his direction. "You want to go there? Want me to tell Nylah how I got traumatized, and you yelled at me?"

He sneered as he hit the steering wheel.

"Or you want me to tell Nylah that you were my hero and saved me? You got me safely home and back to Grim."

"Fucking hell."

"Yeah, I figured."

He stuck out his pierced tongue. "Bite me. But don't. I don't fucking want that shit. Only Nylah gets her teeth on me."

"Ugh. Why do you always have to tell everyone about the weird shit you do in the bedroom? I don't want to know."

"Yeah, you do. It gives you ideas."

Uh, no.

"I can't with you."

"Then don't."

Why the hell did I ever go anywhere with Rael?

"I can't believe that fucker is still alive. We got the wrong fucking asshole. Go figure."

My phone vibrated in my purse, and I checked the screen. "It's Grim."

Rael cringed.

"Hey, babe."

"Are you okay?"

"Yes."

"Unharmed?"

"Yeah, Dex."

"Tell me you didn't leave The Crossroads."

"I didn't leave," I paused, "alone."

"Trish, my angel, my fucking goddess, I am going to spank that ass when I get ahold of you."

"And I'll enjoy it."

"You close?"

"Yes, Rael is driving. You're on speaker."

"I should fucking take your patch, Rael."

Rael swallowed. "I'm fucking sorry, pres. Won't ever happen again. Doesn't matter how much she begs for lube."

"Jesus. Fucking. Christ," Grim growled.

"You want me to lie?"

"Fuck no."

"Then I'm not."

"How far away are you?"

"Three minutes out. Comin' in hot."

"Fine."

"And pres?"

"Fuck. What?"

"We got a big fucking problem."

"Yeah, I know. Razr is alive."

"That's not all. We killed his twin brother," Rael revealed.

"Motherfucker."

ROYAL BASTARDS MC

Chapter 12

GRiM

EVERYTHING WAS FUCKED.

RAZR was fucking alive. Rael let Trish leave The Crossroads. Creed was sick. And I had a club pissed off we reaped the wrong fucking soul.

I had to get out of The Crossroads and ride into the desert. The stress of the last week had built up in my shoulders and neck. I was antsy as fuck. And my Reaper? He fought for control, staying leashed only because I had the will to keep him contained.

For now.

I turned the key and started my bike, dropping my ass onto the seat.

"Going somewhere?"

Mammoth. "To Lucifer."

"Good idea. I'll come with you."

He wasn't asking. I didn't want to argue about it.

"Let's ride."

With a crisp nod, he rode out behind me, following my lead. We rode for several miles until I recognized the bend in the road that led out to where we took the Devil's Ride. It was our club's initiation. How we separated the strong from the weak.

If you could survive Lucifer's tricks and sign his contract in your blood, you had what it took to become a Reaper. He never got far with those that weren't tough or brave enough.

I took the turn, riding with Mammoth as the dust kicked up behind us. We left a trail that soon blew in the hot Nevada wind, dissipating as we rode further inside the Great Basin. Around us, cacti and tumbleweed provided the only shade under an unforgiving sun.

I pulled to a stop and cut the engine, swinging a leg over to stand. Pissed and agitated, I needed answers from the one being that was supposed to help us fight our enemies.

"Lucifer!" I hollered. "Where the fuck are you?"

Mammoth arched a brow. "He might take offense to that."

"He takes offense to everything unless he finds it humorous."

"Even then," Mammoth grunted.

"You kept the truth from us!" I shouted. "What the fuck!?"

He didn't show. The asshole ignored me. *Fucking figures.*

Lucifer should have told us about Razr. Our Reapers sensed something was off, but we didn't know the reason. The devil fucking kept us all in the dark, and it didn't make sense. We were his vessels, his chosen to reap the souls of the wicked and send them to hell. We were the hands of death, molded by Lucifer himself.

"You didn't want to listen."

I spun around and stared into his blood-red eyes. "Not true."

"Yes. I came to your church meeting." He snickered. "I do love the play on words."

Mammoth shook his head.

The devil had the worst ADD at times.

"You didn't tell us shit. I asked," I reminded him.

"And I offered my assistance." He shrugged. "You declined."

Mammoth winced. "He's not wrong."

I glared at my V.P.

"You said you didn't need my help or interference, so I left. Your loss."

Well, fuck.

"I don't think you would have told us anyway, am I right?"

Lucifer smiled. "You'll never know."

"Coming here was pointless." I sighed. "I need to get back to The Crossroads."

"You know, I do appreciate how ruthless and cunning Razr turned out to be. Such a pathetic, sniveling child, and yet he sacrificed his brother without a hint of remorse. How utterly delicious."

Or barbaric. Selfish. Cruel. Narcissistic. I could think of a few other adjectives that worked. I'd seen some dirty shit done to other people before but to hand over your twin brother to take the fall for your shit, dying in your place, was the lowest of the low. No wonder Lucifer thought it was great.

"You are wasting your time with me." The devil snapped his fingers and fucking disappeared.

"I really hate that," Mammoth deadpanned.

"Yeah. Fucker always knows the most annoying moment to do it too."

We rode back home, approaching the gate as Zane opened it. Beside him, Sid stood as if he were waiting for me.

I parked my bike, rising off the seat to stash my helmet and gloves. Once I had them secured in my saddlebags, I faced Sid. Zane remained at his post.

"What is it, kid? I don't have all goddamn day."

"I'll be quick. I'd like to prospect for your club."

"Why?"

"Because I want to be a part of something. To have brothers who care about me and guys I'd do anything for, the same as they'd do for me. I love to ride. Have my own bike, too."

"It's a piece of shit," Rael remarked as he joined us, ticking his head toward the old bike I didn't recognize.

I didn't reply to Rael. He could fuck off. I was pissed at him, and he knew it.

"Not goin' anywhere, pres. I'll take the silent treatment until you love me again."

Christ. "Get me a beer," I bellowed.

Rael grinned. "Sure."

He walked away as I muttered under my breath.

"Well? Can I?"

I almost forgot the kid was here. "It won't be easy."

"I know."

"You need a sponsor. I won't be doing it."

"I will." Bodie's voice surprised me. "I think he deserves a chance."

Fine. "Don't cock it up, Sid. You get one shot. That's it."

He grinned way too damn wide. "I won't."

"You still owe me for my fucking bike."

"I'll work seven days a week."

"Yeah, you will. The next year will kick your ass," Bodie promised. "You answer to me and our president, Grim. Don't fucking call him that until you get permission."

"Okay. I won't let you down."

"Don't ever promise that shit," Bodie corrected. "We all fuck up."

"It's how you fix it that matters," Rael added, joining us as he popped off the top and handed me a cold beer.

I needed to drag this shit out and make Rael my bitch for the next month. He was gonna regret taking Trish from The Crossroads and placing my charming, irreplaceable, persuasive, headstrong woman anywhere without my permission. Fuck that. He was gonna suffer for a long ass time, and I'd love every second of it.

"I'm headin' in to see Trish. Go to Mammoth if you need anything."

My V.P. would ensure I was only bothered if things were serious.

TRiSH

"DADDY!" CREED JUMPED UP from the floor to tackle Grim as he opened the door. "I'm all better!"

Not really. A couple of doses of antibiotics had helped, though. He was feeling much better. But the infection would take ten days to be fully eradicated.

"Grrrr. Ghrowl. G.G."

Grim hugged Creed, picking him up as he joined me on the couch. "I think he likes to growl at me because I'm such a badass."

It was a joke, but maybe he was right. Creed admired his father. He might be young, but he was brilliant. He understood Grim and the club members were different. I could tell. With the innocence of a child, he accepted them without fear.

I lowered my chin and touched my nose to Creed's and nuzzled him. "Are you Ghrowl?"

He shook his head.

"Is Daddy?"

"No, Mama. Silly."

Creed poked Grim in the chest. "Grrrr."

"Daddy is Grrrr?"

Creed beamed a grin. "Yes!"

G.G., Ghrowl, and Grrrr. Three separate beings? Or did G.G. mean Ghrowl and Grrrr?

I finally got it. It clicked. "Grim, let the Reaper say hi to Creed."

He flicked his gaze to mine as his brows furrowed. "You sure?"

"Yeah. I want to test something."

Grim's face transformed, and his Reaper pushed through, allowing enough of his presence to be recognized. The bony structure and monstrous features appeared, far too clear in the light of day. Equal parts fascinating and frightening.

"Ghrowl!" Creed shouted, clapping his hands. "Daddy! Ghrowl."

The Reaper laughed. "He knows my name."

Wait. The Reaper had a name? Why didn't I think of that before now?

"You are mine," he rumbled, grasping my chin before kissing me. Warm lips devoured my mouth, seeking entrance as his tongue pushed inside. It ended far too quickly. "As the child is also mine." His hand lowered to my stomach. "You will give me another soon."

Oh. Wow. How did he know that?

Was I pregnant already?

The Reaper's lips twitched. "Not yet."

Ohhhhhh. I could feel my cheeks heating from a blush. He meant he would be practicing until it happened.

"Beautiful." His fingers brushed the skin on my face. "Ours to protect. To cherish. To fuck," he revealed, lowering his voice.

Yes, I understood what all that meant. It was still odd sometimes to comprehend that Grim shared space with the Reaper. Not just any Reaper. The Grim.

They really were two different beings who shared his body. And I honestly didn't mind because I got both of them.

"I'm yours. Both of you," I agreed.

The Reaper loved to hear it. He craved it. Desire flared in his molten gaze.

"So you're Ghrowl."

"Yes."

"Creed loves you. You play together at night, don't you?"

"Often. Never fear. I will always keep him safe."

"But Grim is sleeping."

"A child can see what adults can't. He's innocent. Untainted."

My boy saw spirits? That sounded like a burden, not to mention scary. "So he can see with the spirit?"

"Yesssss," Ghrowl admitted. "Never the harmful ones."

Wow. "That's amazing. Thank you. For protecting him."

Ghrowl's warm breath tickled my ear as he shifted, lowering his head so only I could hear. "Share me later. Let me come to you. I'll pleasure you with my tongue and cock until you beg me to stop."

My heart thudded in my chest as I felt arousal bloom in my core, tingling my pussy as I clenched my thighs together.

"I can smell it. You're already wet for me."

"Grim." I cleared my throat when he hissed. "Ghrowl."

"Yes, beautiful mate?"

"I want you both."

"You will always have us."

When he backed away, the look on his face, the burning need in his eyes, nearly made me come on the spot. What a wicked, sensual creature.

He winked and receded, allowing Grim to return.

"Babe. That was fucking wild."

Of course, Grim knew almost everything that happened with his Reaper. The only absence of connection was when Ghrowl spirit walked with Creed. Fascinating.

The idea of being with both at the same time intrigued me but also turned me on. We hadn't gotten that far yet. Maybe Ghrowl waited for the right moment.

"All the Reapers have names," Grim announced with awe. "We never considered it, but we should have. They are separate beings. Mammoth has Helkin. I have Ghrowl."

"Bet Rael's is something crazy," I joked.

"Like Asshole," Grim grunted.

"You love him. He's one of your closest brothers in the club."

"He's still an asshole."

I couldn't argue with that.

ROYAL BASTARDS MC

Chapter 13

GRiM

M<small>Y</small> R<small>EAPER</small> <small>SENSED</small> R<small>AZR'S</small> presence outside The Crossroads before I had a chance to hear the rumble of his motorcycle. He rode alone. One rider. Razr thought he could beat me one on one. Fucking clueless. His arrogance would be his downfall.

I kissed Trish, ordered her to remain upstairs with Creed, and rushed outside, shoving my gun behind my back and tucking the weapon where I could quickly grab it. Not that I would need it. The Reaper would react before I needed to use it.

Razr sat on a Harley outside the gate, facing The Crossroads. "Come out and face me, Grim. We've fucked around long enough."

Agreed. Time to find out the truth, motherfucker.

Mammoth's hand landed on my shoulder. "Give him hell."

Rael ticked his chin toward Razr. "He fucked around, let him find out."

My Reaper agreed. I pulled my gun from behind my back and slapped it into Mammoth's hand. "Hold on to that for me."

Razr sneered. "Not worried I'll put a bullet through your brain? Sloppy."

What a fool. His bullshit had gone on long enough.

I didn't give him a chance to reject what was coming or ride off. I ran toward the gate as Zane pulled it open, unleashed my Reaper to let him gain control, and plucked Razr from his seat.

His eyes bulged as he dangled in the air, reaching for my wrist as his feet kicked and he knocked over his bike. It fell over with a crash. "What the hell?"

Ghrowl took control, holding his enemy suspended in the air. I knew my face had taken on his form when Razr began flailing his arms and legs. Panic filled his eyes.

"What the fuck are you!?"

"Vengeance," Ghrowl replied.

He shook Razr so hard his teeth clicked together, and his neck nearly snapped. "I will bleed you so slowly it takes days to die." The odor of urine saturated the air, and Ghrowl chuckled.

He called his first companion. "Shred."

Jigsaw's Reaper stepped forward with a salacious grin. "You've taken from us, so we'll take our pound of flesh from *you*."

Razr screamed as wounds began to open on his skin, tiny cuts slicing into his bare arms and legs as blood soaked into his clothes. One slice appeared above his right eye and began to drip down his temple.

"Devourer," Ghrowl called next.

Exorcist's Reaper joined us. He laughed as he began to consume Razr's soul while it was still attached to his body. The horror of it, the agony, sent chills down my spine.

Patriot moved forward. "His fear is delicious."

"Feed," Ghrowl encouraged, and Patriot closed his eyes, swaying as he pulled on Razr's spirit, conjuring frightening images that only increased his terror.

Razr's body twitched and jolted. Endless groans escaped as his eyes grew glassy. His focus disappeared as he was lost to the images only he could see.

When Razr reached his limit of human suffering, Ghrowl ordered them all to stand back. I resumed control.

"Mammoth, Wraith, Bodie, Chaos, and Diablo. You know what to do."

Razr rolled into the fetal position, whimpering as they walked to their motorcycles. As if one shared mind, they sat on their bikes, started the engines, and moved into position.

One bike and rider at each location. Five points. Razr's head, each arm, and both legs. Rope secured each limb and neck, connecting Razr's body to each of the five Reapers and their rides.

Shock must have taken hold because Razr said nothing. An occasional twitch indicated he still breathed. He lay on his back as I squatted next to his piss-soaked, bloody body.

"You should have run when you had the chance. Now, you'll live in hell for all eternity. A meal for the devil to consume as you experience the agony of being eaten and digested repeatedly for the remainder of time."

Razr blinked. He was close to death but not so far gone to miss the meaning of my words. "Mercy."

"You offered none to others in your short, pathetic life. None will be granted to you. You now reap what you have sown. Any eye for an eye. Vindication." I paused. "Reaper style."

I stood as Ghrowl seamlessly moved into position, the scythe glistening in the hot Nevada sun as I held it in my hand. "This soul is mine."

The club stood in silent support as I nodded to the riders. They revved their engines, popped wheelies, and then pulled back on their throttles. Each bike shot forward. The ropes pulled tight, ripping into flesh and muscle as Razr was yanked in five different directions at the same time.

Right before he died, I reaped his soul. His spirit disconnected from his body as his filmy essence hovered above the ground in front of me, already torn from Exorcist's feast.

His eyes widened as he watched his physical body torn apart and scattered across the desert sand. The riders would drag his remains through the Great Basin until none remained—nothing but bits and pieces for the scavengers to devour. No part of him would ever be found.

His mouth opened in a silent scream. The extent of his suffering was too great for a single sound to echo. He deserved every second of it before his death.

The ground began to rumble beneath my feet. It quaked and grumbled, cracking open and popping with hissing thirst. The fires of hell blew hot as they erupted, burning the filaments of Razr's soul. Each piece began to ignite, burning with the stench of sulfur.

I felt the presence of every Reaper join me. They wanted to reap his soul and pass judgment as one. The club suffered together, and now it would finally receive retribution as one entity. Every scythe swiped through his filmy, stinky soul at once. We shredded him as we hovered above the ground, destroying what remained until nothing but tiny flickers and ashes fell into the open fissures below.

Loud slurping sounds below our feet proved Razr had been received. Cries of horror and pain rose as the flames angrily sparked in shades of green, orange, and red. The fires burned brighter for a moment before simmering low. The ground slowly began to close. The fissures smoothed out.

Within a minute, no hint of hell's entrance remained.

And nothing of Razr was left to bury, mourn, or remember.

Rael stood next to me, holding onto a pike. I had no idea where he found it. "I was gonna place his head on here and let you swing a bat at it. It could have been fun."

I snorted. "Maybe."

"But we waited long enough. We'll just find another sick fuck to put on the pike."

"Rael."

"Yeah, pres?"

"Give me a hug, you sick fuck."

He laughed, slapped my back, and then his smile disappeared.

It sank in as he backed away. "Now, pres, I said I was sorry about Trish."

"And if you let your Reaper take control, you won't feel much pain."

Rael turned to Mammoth. "Is he serious?"

Mammoth tried to hide his humor. "Yeah, I think so."

"Better run, Rael," I warned.

He took off, got about ten steps away, and then stopped. "Shit. You had me there for a minute."

I sure did. "Don't ever change, brother."

Rael sauntered back to my side. "Never, pres."

ROYAL BASTARDS MC

Chapter 14

TRiSH

"M<small>ATE."</small>

T<small>HE SEDUCTIVE PURR</small> of Grim's voice awakened me early in the morning, long before the sun dared to peek over the horizon. Meager light filtered into the room and brightened enough that I could see the expression of the man who gazed into my eyes.

Wait. Not Grim. Ghrowl.

The Reaper sought me out, not my sexy biker.

"Ghrowl."

He lowered his head, peppering kisses along my jaw, stopping to nibble on the flesh of my earlobe. "He gave you a son."

Ghrowl meant Dex—the president of the club.

"I want to give you a child. Boy or girl. I don't care which."

I sucked in a breath. "Is that possible?"

"Oh, yes."

"Would the baby still be Grim's?"

"Of course. Creed is my son, too."

Good point.

"Is that why Creed is special?" I knew there was something different about him. My boy could sense things. He was sensitive to the Reapers.

"One of many reasons."

"Will I ever learn them all?"

"Someday, yes." He kissed down my neck, flicking his tongue out to lick down the column of my throat. "I want to devour you."

That sounded exciting, intriguing, and a little scary.

"Never fear me." His head lifted. Silver shined in the gray of Grim's eyes. "I am your protector. I will never allow pain unless you beg for it." A smirk twitched his lips. "Please beg if you feel the need."

God. That husky, deep timbre was almost identical to Grim, but something darker hid underneath, igniting a spark of desire that began to simmer low in my core.

Ghrowl made a sound that reminded me of a purr. A sound that a lion might make when he wished to soothe his mate. I bet lions felt frisky after that.

I sure did. The sound resonated deep inside, and my legs fell open wide enough to allow Grim's body to fill the empty void. Wedged snugly in the cradle of my hips, Ghrowl began to roll his hips. Every time he pressed into me, I felt his erection bumping into my clit.

Good God. That friction felt incredible.

He reached for my wrists, pinning them above my head. "I'm going to tear off your clothes, lick your pussy, and fuck you hard. Sound good, my beautiful goddess?"

Um, yes. So much, yes.

I eagerly nodded.

Ghrowl reached for my clothes and began ripping the material, shredding the tank top and panties I wore to bed after I tucked in Creed, too tired to strip. I usually slept naked, but this sure made me change my mind as I watched the feral twist of his mouth and the blatant lust in his eyes.

The tattered pieces of material hung loose as Ghrowl inched lower, slowly retreating down the bed until his head was level with my pussy. He didn't hesitate to grip my hips and lift me up, keeping me suspended as his wicked tongue began to slide through my slit. He licked along my entrance, devouring me as he alternated sucking on my clit to teasing my opening, only lowering me to glide two of his fingers inside.

I gasped, pumping my hips to his eager rhythm, far too gone in rapture to care about the sounds that fell from my lips.

"Don't stop," he growled. "Keep telling me how good it feels."

Coherent thought fled. I couldn't think. I didn't notice the world around me. All I knew and felt was Ghrowl, my Grim, and the orgasm building into such a frenzy I thought I would combust.

A deep purr fell from Ghrowl's mouth as he settled his lips over my clit, rubbing and teasing the nub. I never felt anything like this. I couldn't fight it. I didn't want it to stop.

When I came, I knew I cried out his name, shouting it with my release as I humped Ghrowl's face. He leaned back, licking the taste of me from his lips.

"I want that again. Soon."

Oh, me too.

"I need to be inside you."

"Then fuck me, Ghrowl," I begged. "I need you."

A fierce longing swept over his face before he positioned the tip of his cock at my entrance. "I've waited for this."

"For me?"

"Yes."

"Why?" I asked, truly curious.

"For you to know which of your males is fucking and loving you."

My heart clenched as Ghrowl pushed forward, thrusting hard to lodge deep inside me. He didn't move, pausing to let me feel the engorged length of him. God. Was it possible that he felt even larger than usual?

"I've swollen with need. I'm going to fill you so full my seed will take. I want to watch your belly grow, knowing I put the child in your womb."

He sounded so utterly possessive, cocky, but also undeniably committed.

"Ghrowl."

"You are mine. I share you, but you must learn I am yours, too. Two males to protect and cherish you."

When he put it like that, I knew I was a lucky woman.

"How often do I get to have you?" I asked, wondering if he would only bond with me like this when he wanted me to conceive.

A dark frown shadowed his features. "Every night. Whenever you wish. Say my name, and I will come to you. Grim has already conceded that you will want us both."

He did? I blinked, feeling guilty. "I don't want to hurt him."

"Not possible. We may be separate beings, but we share the heart in his body. It beats to please you."

This was so bizarre.

Ghrowl slowly began to move, rocking his hips as he slid in and out of me. His palms fell on the mattress on either side of my body as he began to pick up the pace, gathering speed as his thrusts grew bolder and deeper.

I had to touch him. My fingertips grazed his arms, rising to caress his chest and abdominal muscles.

Ghrowl jolted, shuddering as I slid around his hips to hold onto his ass. The man had a perfect backside.

"I want to ruin you. Claim you. Erase the memory of every sexual encounter before Grim."

"Then do it. Ruin me. Claim me. I'm yours."

The sounds of our bodies meeting filled the room. Sweat began to cling to our skin. All too soon, I felt my orgasm building to the point I couldn't hold it back.

"Come," he ordered with a grunt.

"Ghrowl!"

I knew I clenched him hard when he hissed, pumping fast, driving into me when my release exploded through my lower body. I felt the sheets damped beneath us.

"My Trish," he rasped, rutting until his body slammed into mine and held me down. He emptied into me, staring into my eyes as his hips snapped multiple times. With the last spurt, he held me in place. "Don't move," he huffed, his chest meeting mine as he slowed his breathing.

Wow. That was intense.

"Are you okay?"

"Yes."

"This was good?"

I blinked. The Reaper Ghrowl wanted to know if I had a good time as he fucked me? Adorable. "Oh, yes. I loved it."

A satisfied smile curved his lips. "I want to fuck again tomorrow night."

Uh-huh. "Me too."

"And the night after that." His mouth lowered, skillfully kissing me until my toes almost curled. "And every night."

"So you're addicted?"

"Fucking you is my new favorite thing to do."

Well, Reapers didn't hold back, did they?

"You're bold."

"For you, yes."

"It's a good thing I'm bold for both of you too."

Ghrowl finally pulled out of me, still partially rigid. He said that mating me would keep him ready to go most of the time for months if not years. Reapers loved to fuck. I guess I would benefit a lot from that.

Humored, I rested my head on his chest. When our combined fluids began to drip out of me, he used his fingers to slowly push them back in, giving me a grin so heated that we ended up going a second round.

I fell asleep as he held me.

"My Trish."

Whispering woke me up, but I didn't move or open my eyes.

"I love you, babe. For you, I would risk everything. My club. My patch. My fucking soul. There's no world I could live in where you weren't with me."

Oh, Grim.

"I know," I answered.

"And sharing you with Ghrowl is a compromise I'm happy with because it means you're always loved, protected, and cared for. He longs to be with you, and I feel that bond. It's connected us on a deeper level."

"I feel that too," I admitted.

"Good. I love you, Trish." His hand lowered to my belly. "We're gonna be happy, babe. That's our future. Me, you, and all our babies."

Our family.

At one time, I never thought this was possible. Now, I believed Grim. We had a fantastic future, and I planned to enjoy every second of it with my G.G.

ROYAL BASTARDS MC

Epilogue

TRiSH

NINE MONTHS LATER

"How do you think the guys are doing?" I asked, trying not to moan as the masseuse rubbed my swollen feet. "I'm still not convinced they could handle all the kids alone."

Sasha snorted. "Bodie is probably covered in markers and crumbs from Maverick's snacks."

"I bet Rael fell asleep," Nylah laughed. "The twins exhaust him."

"Gavin and Gage are a handful like Creed," I agreed. "Do you think we'll walk into a disaster?"

"Without a doubt," Mimi agreed. She pressed her hands to her chest. "I need to pump. My breastmilk supply is crazy good, but I leak like a faucet all the damn time."

She was thrilled, though. I could see it. "Patriot is so happy to have another son, especially a child that shares his DNA."

"He's already talking about trying for another one."

"So is Bodie," Sasha sighed. "I love that he's so enthusiastic."

"Oh, they have no problem with that," Bess agreed. "Papa just wants to practice all the time."

Giggles erupted around the room. Yeah, we talked about this while we all lounged on massage tables. Who cared what other people thought? We didn't. The Ol' Ladies weren't going to censor our conversation just because we were in public. The only exception to that was any talk of the Reapers or club details.

We finished our afternoon at the spa and headed home. I could barely stand on my own, and Sasha laughed as she helped me get out of the car.

"You look like you're going to go into labor any minute."

"Tell that to my cervix," I deadpanned. I was a week beyond my due date. My baby boy didn't want to come out and meet his brother yet.

"I think you should say that to Grim."

Ha. Or Ghrowl. He would enjoy trying to bring on my labor through sex. Grim would worry too much.

Colorful lights were strung up outside around the covered picnic area and the roof of The Crossroads. The festive décor made me smile. I loved this time of year.

Grim ordered Rael to put up the inflatable biker Santa Claus with several presents, a snowman, and a few reindeer. He also had to decorate the inside with the prospects. Nine months after Rael took me to the pharmacy after Grim ordered me to stay at The Crossroads because of Razr's threats, he still had to do shit for Grim. Rael managed to stay on his president's shit list the whole year.

Most of the guys got a kick out of seeing Rael grovel. Grim never relented.

We headed inside . . .and into chaos.

Wrapping paper, tape, and rolls of ribbon were scattered across the floor. Food scraps. Crumbs. Candy wrappers.

Holiday cookies from the bake-off we had recently. Open bags of chips and pretzels. Multiple strands of lights, some plugged in and twinkling. Others were unlit. Bows had been pressed all over the common room on furniture, kids, and some of the club members. A few toys and unwrapped presents were now on display. Two games were open. One already had pieces missing.

The only thing I didn't see? Alcohol.

All of the dads looked dazed, slumped back on several of the leather couches. Not a child remained awake. They had all probably crashed from the sugar rush.

"What in the actual fuck?" I asked as my gaze slid over Grim.

He opened his mouth and then shut it.

Rael shrugged, a look of defeat on his features as he snuck a glance at Nylah.

Bodie held his son and pretended to nod off.

Patriot scratched the back of his neck. He finally leaned back, accepting defeat after Mimi's glare.

Papa was the only man left standing. He ate popcorn from a bowl, tossing buttered pieces into his mouth. "I arrived in time for this shit show. I'm plannin' to watch how it ends."

Bess shook her head, amused.

"I asked for one night, Dex."

He cringed. "My goddess, the love of my life."

Rael snickered.

Patriot cuffed him on the back of the head.

"Ow. Fuck."

I rolled my eyes. Would Rael ever grow up?

"I want this cleaned up by morning."

Grim nodded. "It'll get done."

"Not the prospects either."

Bodie sighed. "We're fucked."

Yeah, probably.

"Babe, why don't you go put your feet up."

I opened my mouth to reply when I felt a sharp pain in my stomach, and then it hardened. Oh, ouch. My eyes slid shut as I breathed through the contraction, recognizing what my body was doing since I'd gone through it already with Creed.

There was a tiny pop, and then fluid gushed out of me in front of everyone. A clear puddle appeared below my feet. My water broke!

Grim was at my side as my eyes opened, searching his face.

"Babe, our son is finally coming."

"Yeah," I agreed. "Finally."

He grinned. "We need to get to the hospital."

"It's an hour away."

"That's why we're leaving now."

Grim began shouting orders as people scrambled. Parents rushed to their kids. Club members hopped to do their president's bidding. I felt my world tip as Grim picked me up.

"Hey, my mate."

Ghrowl.

"Yes?"

"Time to meet our baby." He winked.

I clutched my belly as another contraction started.

Merry Christmas, little one.

I hope you enjoyed the second part of Grim and Trish's story.

If you're new to the Tonopah, NV Royal Bastards MC, start with *The Biker's Gift*.

You can read the next book in the Tonopah, NV chapter, *A Crossroads Christmas*, December 2024.

Xenon finally gets his story in February 2025 in *Sinfully Mine*.

The first book in the Vegas Chapter is *Hell on Wheels*, following Maddog, the new president. It's available now.

Book 4 in the Vegas chapter, *Rattlin' Bones*, releases October 2024.

Find all Nikki's Royal Bastards MC books on Amazon and Kindle Unlimited.

Never miss out on a book! Follow Nikki on social media to receive updates.

You can find her links here:

https://linktr.ee/nikkilandis

REAPER MÉTIER

Grim Reaper – Aurabarer

Mammoth – Gravitor/Myokinetic

Rael – Berserker

Chrome – Elementalist

Exorcist – Soulripper

Jigsaw – Eviscerator

Wraith – Ghostwalker

Hannibal – Souleater

Patriot – Fearmonger

Chaos – Firewielder

Papa – Soulwithren

Bodie – Heartsunder

Bones – Chainbinder

Diablo – Bloodreader

Xenon – TBD

Toad – Renderscream

Shadow – Shadoweaver

Spook – Soulseer/Timespinner

Zane – TBD

#1 The Biker's Gift

#2 Bloody Mine

#3 Ridin' for Hell

#4 Devil's Ride

#5 Hell's Fury

#6 Grave Mistake

#7 Papa Noel

#8 The Biker's Wish

#9 Eternally Mine

#10 Twisted Devil

#11 Violent Bones

#12 Haunting Chaos

#13 Santa Biker

#14 Viciously Mine

#15 Jigsaw's Blayde

#16 Spook's Possession

#17 Infinitely Mine

#18 Grim Justice

#19 A Crossroads Christmas

#20 Sinfully Mine

#21 TBD

TONOPAH, NV CHAPTER

Pres/Founder – Grim Reaper

VP/Founder – Mammoth

SGT at Arms – Azrael, Angel of Death "Rael"

Enforcer – Exorcist

Enforcer – Jigsaw

Secretary – Wraith

Treasurer – Hannibal

Road Captain – Patriot

Tail Gunner – Chaos

Founder – Papa

Member – Bodie

Member – Bones

Member – Chrome

Member/Cleaner – Diablo

Member/Tech – Xenon

Member – Shadow

Member – Toad

Member – Spook

Prospect – Zane

Prospect – Sid

Royal Bastards MC Las Vegas, NV
#1 Hell on Wheels
#2 Reckless Mayhem (Manic Parts 1 & 2)
#3 Jeepers Creepers
#4 Rattlin' Bones
Mayhem Makers: Manic Mayhem (Manic Part 1)

LAS VEGAS, NV CHAPTER

Pres – Maddog

V.P. – Skeletor

SGT at Arms – Manic

Enforcer – Creature

Nomad/Enforcer – Darius "The Jackal"

Secretary – Crusher

Treasurer – Dice

Road Captain – Hex

Tail Gunner – Slash

Member/Cleaner – Tombstone

Member/Tech – Snapshot

Chaplain – Testament

JUSTICE

Playlist

And So It Went (feat. Tom Morello) – The Pretty Reckless

Scarlet Cross – Black Veil Brides

Obsolete – Of Mice & Men

Heart of a Champion (feat. Papa Roach & Ice Nine Kills)

Breathe Again – Pop Evil

Obey (with YUNGBLUD) – Bring Me The Horizon

Mercy – Ayron Jones

For the Glory – All Good Things

The Unknown – 10 Years

Heavy Is The Crown – Daughtry

Right Now – Korn

Born for Greatness – Papa Roach

A Conversation with Death – Khemmis

Someone – Aaron Lewis

Run On (feat. King Sugar) – Jamie Bower

Bad Man – Disturbed

The Hangman – War Hippies

Hole In Your Head – Ekoh

Can't Walk On the Water – Blake Tyler

Judgment Day – Five Finger Death Punch

You can listen to Nikki's Playlists on Spotify.

One Hell of a ride!

Royal Bastards MC, founded in 2019.

Royal Bastards MC Facebook Group -
https://www.facebook.com/groups/royalbastardsmc/

Website - https://www.royalbastardsmc.com/

6th Run

Kristine Dugger: Crazy Psycho

KL Ramsey: Lost in Yonkers

Barbara Nolan: Loving Smoke

Crimson Syn: Tormented by Regret

Elizabeth N. Harris: Warden

Liberty Parker: Butcher's Destruction

Morgan Jane Mitchell: Hard Knox

B.B. Blaque: Royal Family

Darlene Tallman: Kraken's Release

H.J. Marshall: Roughstock

Claire Shaw: Tyres

Kathleen Kelly: Highway

J. Lynn Lombard: Jaded Red

India R. Adams: Praying for Fire

Nikki Landis: Grim Justice

Dani René: REV

Verlene Landon: Snagged by Hook

Kris Anne Dean: Scorched Souls

J.L. Leslie: Worth it All

Jena Doyle: Blood and Whiskey

K.D. Latronico: Wherever I May Roam

Sapphire Knight: Toxic Biker

Nicole James: Taking What's Ours

Rae B. Lake: Sins and Paradise

Kristine Allen: Blade

Roux Cantrell: Hell Bent

Daphne Loveling: Deadly North

M Merin: Big Timber

Amy Davies: Seized by Solo

J.A. Collard: In Too Deep

Elle Boon: Royally Embraced

Murphy Wallace: Misery and Ecstasy

Theta James: Demon in the Shadows

Chelle C. Craze & Eli Abbott

Love motorcycle romance?

Check out these books by Nikki Landis:

Feral Rebels MC/Royal Bastards MC Crossover

#1 Claimed by the Bikers

#2 One Night with the Bikers

#3 Snowed In with the Bikers

Reaper's Vale MC/Royal Bastards MC Crossover

#1 Twisted Iron

#2 Savage Iron

Devil's Murder MC

#1 Crow

#2 Raven

#3 Hawk

#4 Talon

#5 Crow's Revenge

#6 Heron

#7 Cuckoo

#8 Claw

#9 Carrion

#10 TBD

Night Striders MC
#1 Rebel Road
#2 Ravaged Road
#3 Vengeful Road

Saint's Outlaws MC
Prequel: My Christmas Biker
#1 Brick's Redemption
#2 TBD

Kings of Anarchy MC Ohio
#1 Property of Scythe
#2 Property of Mountain
#3 TBD

Summit Hill Vipers
#1 My Stepbrother Biker
#2 My Tattooed Hitchhiker
#3 My Ex-Boyfriend Stalker
#4 My Hero Biker
#5 TBD
Mayhem Makers: My Inked Neighbor

Iron Renegades MC
#1 Roulette Run
#2 Jester's Ride
#3 Surviving Saw
Origins: Ground Zero

Ravage Riders MC
#1 Sins of the Father
#2 Sinners & Saints
#3 Sin's Betrayal
#4 Life of Sin
#5 Born Sinner

SNEAK PEEK

MY
STEPBROTHER
BIKER

GAGE

I DIDN'T LIE WHEN I told Letty on the night of the wedding that I'd be seeing her around, but I also didn't confide that she wouldn't be having any contact with me during those two years.

And now, after the long wait, I finally had permission to reappear in her life.

My right knee wouldn't stop bouncing as I tapped my thigh, eager for church to end. Storm sent me a look as he noticed, and it distracted him. Shit. I crossed my arms over my chest and leaned back, stretching out my legs under the table in the center of the room. The club's logo stretched across the surface, etched into the wood. The same emblem I wore on the back of my cut.

I prospected for this club in high school and patched in the summer after I graduated. The men gathered around this table were family. Not a soul related to me by blood. That didn't matter in my world. We were brothers, bonded through our allegiance to the club and our way of life.

A concept my father would never understand. The only thing he recognized was dollar signs.

I focused on Storm's words, refusing to steal a glance at my phone to check the time.

"Boomer, Wolf, get your asses to that meeting. We need eyes and ears on that shit. Don't get seen and cock it up."

They nodded, rising from the table to head out.

Blendcore Enterprises, my father's company, merged corporations and sold goods and companies, whatever they could get their greedy hands on. Lately, that included weapons that supplied our enemies. We needed more intel and the only way to get it included spying on meetings between our rival club and the mediator from Blendcore.

"You sure that dancer from Show 'N' Tail got the info right?" Cash asked, flicking ash from his cigarette onto a tray. "Ain't doubting your word, pres. Just lookin' out."

Storm grunted. "Yeah, she's good for it. No love for the fuckers at Blendcore. They bought out the company that owned her apartment building and had her evicted."

Damn. "Fuck," I cursed, shaking my head. I hated hearing this shit. My father was ruthless, and his reputation was confirmed every time we learned something new.

"This ain't on you, Blade," Storm reminded me. "We've been over this shit."

Yeah, I knew. "I still don't like it."

Cash gripped my shoulder, giving it a shake. "He's his own man, just like you. Let it roll off."

He was right. I nodded, giving Storm an anxious look.

"Church is dismissed. Get the fuck out of here," Storm ordered. His gaze fixed on me as I stood. "Blade," he growled.

"Yeah, pres?" I asked, anxious as fuck to get out the door.

"I know what these last two years cost you. It didn't escape my notice."

I dipped my chin, acknowledging his words.

"Not been easy for you, son, but things are about to change. Keep Letty safe. Whatever, however."

Wow. I slapped my hand over my chest. "Thank you, pres."

"You understand why I had to do it, right?"

His order. The one that kept me from the girl I loved for two fucking years. The agony of it burned in my gut.

"I see you, Blade. I fucking know it hurt, but she was sixteen. Fucking *sixteen*, and you were almost nineteen. Had to keep you clear of that shit."

"I know." I hated it. I would have been with her the whole time. Would that have placed her in additional danger? I couldn't say. My protection never wavered. From the moment I left that wedding, I kept an eye on Letty. If I wasn't around, I asked another prospect. She never went without me or one of my guys. No one fucked with my girl.

And no one *fucked* my girl. I made sure of that.

"I hear you, pres."

Cash sighed. "The shit with her mom and your dad, it had to stay clear from both of you. It was necessary."

"Yeah." They weren't wrong, but I wish I could have explained before I walked away. I left Letty with vague comments and a promise she didn't understand.

And then, this morning, our rival threatened Mifflin and his family. The Crimson Heretics felt cheated by Mifflin's latest deal, pinching off a considerable percentage of their profits. Pissed, their president sent two of his men, who gunned down Mifflin's secretary and left him a package that included her severed hand and a warning. A photo of Cynthia and Letty splashed with blood.

How did we know?

Because Candy Cane, the stripper from Show 'N' Tail, had a magical pussy that seemed to keep Mifflin addicted. He liked to talk to her, thinking she kept his secrets. She never did.

Funny enough, Candy Cane had a thing for Storm. Whatever he wanted, she did. Only with Storm, she knew better than ever to try to betray him.

So, here I stood, waiting for permission to get to my girl. Sure, a prospect arrived at the high school stadium in case shit went down before I could come, but I hated the delay.

"Pres," I pleaded.

He ticked his chin toward the door. "Go. You keep me informed. Got it?"

"Yeah, pres!" I shouted, running out of the goddamn door like my ass was on fire.

Just the idea of being close to Letty again, speaking to her, and breathing the same fucking air pulsed a need in me so fucking deep that I didn't know how I would stay in control once I had a chance to touch her. The ride on my Harley took fifteen minutes. Way too fucking long.

I almost missed her fucking graduation. I arrived in time to see her step onto the stage, relieved to confirm she was alive, unharmed, and as beautiful as ever.

"Leticia Marie Jacobs."

Her name was announced, and she glided across that stage with a smile so fucking huge I clutched my chest to ensure my heart still beat inside it. I waited at the bottom of the stairs, knowing she had to exit where I stood.

She didn't see me at first, but when we touched, she fucking felt the connection. Her head snapped to the side, and her lips parted. Shock flittered over her features.

That's right, baby. I'm back.

Nothing would tear us apart again.

I couldn't keep my hands off her, holding her hand because I needed that contact. I had to feel the warmth and breathe in her sweet scent. My thumb caressed her skin for the remainder of the graduation ceremony. Once it ended, we stood as Cynthia congratulated her daughter.

My focus turned to the mother. Would she stay with Letty and out of trouble?

She slid her gaze across mine, meeting long enough for me to understand that she had to leave. Cynthia hid the shit with Mifflin from her daughter for two years. She tried to protect her and failed. My father only cared about himself. She learned that lesson far too late.

There wasn't a soul he wouldn't sacrifice to stay at the top. That included his wife, son, and stepdaughter.

After we stopped inside the school and the girls picked up their belongings, we walked to the parking lot.

"You're with me," I announced to Letty. "Come on, Beautiful. I'll follow Ava."

I led her toward the black Mustang I borrowed for the day, leaving my bike for the prospect. He'd ride it back to the clubhouse. Tomorrow, I'd switch them out for my bike.

Her eyes widened when she saw the car. "You have a Mustang?"

"Tonight I do."

She stared, unmoving.

"Love, I knew you'd be in a dress and heels. Not exactly the right clothes to ride me."

She arched a brow, caught my meaning, and blushed as pink colored her cheeks. "Ride your bike, you mean."

"Right."

I opened the door, devouring every inch of skin she exposed, and shut it once she had buckled her seatbelt. "What are your plans tonight?" I asked to make conversation once we left the lot.

"Parties." She shrugged. "Probably a lot of them."

Yeah, I figured. I did the same when I graduated, only instead of getting my dick wet, I spent the night wishing she was with me and getting drunk off my ass.

She wouldn't be drinking that much on my watch.

The dinner bored me. My attention kept drifting to Letty's toned, silky legs, and I couldn't keep my hands to myself. I slid my palm over one thigh, hiding my movements underneath the tablecloth. We sat with our backs to the wall, pushed in close enough that no one would see unless they ducked under.

With slow, careful caresses, I rubbed circles over her bare flesh, kneading the soft skin.

Her lips parted, and she tried to pry my hand off, only to find I wouldn't budge.

She was a temptation I couldn't indulge in for so long that now I had no way to fight it. All the time apart increased my need and spiked my lust and desire to new heights, the denial sparking a possessive, obsessive drive that could only be tamed by making her mine. In every fucking way.

"Gage," she whispered, trying to keep the moan out of her voice.

"Yeah, Beautiful?" I asked, sliding my hand to the right, reaching the edge of her panties.

"You can't," she began, gripping the arm of the chair when I slid a finger beneath the fabric, teasing the seam of her slit, daring to push through and find the slick proof of her arousal.

"I can," I growled as I leaned down, whispering into her ear. The loud restaurant blocked us from being heard. "I need a taste."

I pulled my hand back, lifting it without brushing her skin, and went straight to my mouth, sucking on the finger as she stared.

Her pupils blew wide. Lust darkened the shade of blue in her eyes until I stared into sparkling sapphires. *So fucking gorgeous.* I needed to wake up every fucking day to those pretty eyes and that tempting mouth.

"So fucking good," I told her, swirling my tongue before pulling my finger from my mouth, lowering my hand, subtly making my way across her thigh.

This time, she opened wider, letting me have better access.

"So impatient," I murmured, kissing the pulse point below her ear. "Do you think they'll notice when I make you come?"

She gasped. "Gage."

"The taste of you, Beautiful. It's burned into my brain. I can't function without it."

Her legs closed so fast I nearly growled. "And yet you stayed away."

She shoved my hand to the side, and I let her.

"This conversation isn't over, baby." I sat back, picked up my drink, and drained the cup.

"What if I say it is?"

Oh, Beautiful, this isn't a game, but if you want to play, I'll win.

I captured her hand, lifted it above the table, and pressed my lips to the surface, stroking once with my tongue. "Challenge accepted, Beautiful."

Her hand pulled away, but not before I caught the hunger she tried to hide.

Tonight, one way or another, we were hashing this out, preferably with my tongue or lips on her body.

My Stepbrother Biker, **Summit Hill Vipers** releases
April 2025.

SNEAK PEEK
SIN'S BETRAYAL

MACK

T HE NEXT FEW DAYS rolled by without a glitch. Nothing from the Outlaws. No messages from Breaker. As far as I could tell, everything was smooth without a hint of trouble, even from Valan.

A lull of quiet before chaos unleashed.

That was usually when shit went down. None of us were stupid. I'd taken precautions, hoping Valan didn't set up something that could harm the club.

I called for church, slamming down the gavel once all my officers were inside. My son sat on my right, the place reserved for my V.P. as expected. The SGT at Arms position on my left was vacant. Hangman gave me a chin lift, always ready to have my back. He'd be a good choice for S.A.A., but I needed to consider it before I brought the vote to church and the rest of the members. Tank and Halo sat at the opposite end of the table. That left Ghost, the secretary, next to the treasurer, R.J. And last, G.Q. Luke kicked back in his chair, lighting a smoke. As road captain, he constantly plotted the routes we'd take on any ride. He didn't have much to do today, but that would change soon.

"Church is in session, brothers," I announced. "Got to admit, I'm feelin' antsy. It's too fucking quiet."

Edge snorted. "That's how it is. The calm before the storm."

"And that storm is Mack," R.J. joked.

Ghost snickered. "Truth."

"I don't like it," Hangman announced. "There's too much tension and bad blood for the Outlaws to sit on this for long."

"I agree with you," Halo added. "This isn't good."

"We need to be prepared. The club should be on lockdown, pres," Edge advised.

"Already on it," I replied. "Until Breaker is no longer a threat and shit is settled with Bryce, the club is at risk."

"What about Charlotte?" R.J. asked, staring right into my eyes. "She's the sister of my ol' lady. Family. We need to keep her safe."

"And she will be," I declared, trying to remain calm. "That's why we're going into lockdown. To keep the women and kids safe."

A few of my brothers nodded.

Edge spoke up. "Rae is due in less than six weeks. I want to keep her comfortable and limit her stress. It's not good for my son."

"That's why Cara and Charlotte and the girls will be around. They can do girly shit together," R.J. informed us all with a chuckle.

"The club girls need to stay put. No runnin' around or makin' trouble. Ghost, I want you keepin' them in line."

"No problem, pres."

"Hangman, Halo, bring your ol' ladies and kids. I want them secure in case shit goes down."

"You got it," Halo agreed.

Hangman frowned. "Meg is on that fucking book signing cruise, remember? She won't be back for another week."

"Fuck. I forgot. If shit ain't resolved by then, she comes here from the airport."

"I'll be picking her up. She knows how shit works."

Hangman and Meg were high school sweethearts. Nearly twenty years later, they still only had eyes for one another. That was love right there. Waking up every morning to the same face and never wanting that to change.

I wondered if Charlotte was a forever girl, not because she needed security as a single mother but because she wanted to be with her guy until she died. From what I knew of her, I had confidence that the answer was yes. The thought increased my longing to claim her as my ol' lady.

"Glad I'm single," Tank observed. "This shit is stressful."

A couple of the other brothers agreed, including Wolf.

"We need to increase security." Edge ticked his chin my way. "What you want us to do, pres?"

This had already been decided by me, Edge, Ghost, and R.J. but we went through the information for the rest of the club.

"Keep the front gates closed at all times—no one in or out without my or Edge's approval. Keep the prospects on watch, rotating shifts. That means we're all pitchin' in. I don't want to hear shit about it, either. The last thing we need is the Outlaws showin' up while our pants are down and fucking us in the ass. Feel me?"

A few chuckles erupted around the room. No one said a word to contradict me.

"Edge, I want you handling the rotations. Anyone has an issue, and it goes to the V.P. before me. It comes to me, and no one will like my response."

"Alright, pres." Edge gave me a smirk. Smartass probably wanted to call me pops, but he wasn't doing that in church.

"Halo, get with R.J. and ensure we have plenty of supplies. Check over the inventory. If we need anything, take care of it, but fill me in if you've got to leave the compound."

"No problem," R.J. announced, lighting up a smoke. "I can work on that when I'm not getting Cara to relax."

Shaking my head, I didn't reply. She was pregnant, too, but mainly in the early stage, which meant she was sick often.

Halo ticked his chin my way. "Anything specific you want me to stock?"

"Ammo. Water. Food. Ass wipe. All the necessary shit."

His lips curled upward in amusement. "I'll make sure the shitters are stocked."

"You better," G.Q. announced. "Tank clogs that motherfucker every damn day. Add a new fucking plunger to the list. I tossed the other one out. Too many goddamn swishes. The rubber was eroding."

"Fuck off," Tank blurted. "My shit isn't gonna break down rubber."

I couldn't help laughing, along with everyone at the table. These fucking assholes. Never a dull moment.

"I want you all checkin' in with Edge and me with any new information. Tank and Wolf, you're going on recon. Need you to check out the SOMC properties and tell me if you see movement or anything suspicious. It may help to warn us of trouble."

They nodded in unison.

"Jake, I've got some shit for you to look up. You still tinkering on that laptop of yours?"

Jake smirked. "Yeah, pres."

He'd gotten good at the tech stuff. "Good." I handed him a sheet of paper with notes I'd made on it. "I want to dig into the SOMC financials. Valan's shit too. He betrayed us. He doesn't have privacy anymore."

No one disputed that.

"I'm on it, pres," Jake promised.

"I don't want anyone going rogue or anything else stupid right now. We keep this shit tight. Feel me?"

A chorus of "aye" erupted around the table as I ended church.

"CHARLOTTE, I NEED TO speak with you a moment," I announced, poking my head inside one of the private rooms where the ol' ladies liked to hang out and play dominoes. They usually kept the minibar stocked for mixed drinks and the fridge with their snacks. The brothers knew to leave that area alone.

No one wanted to piss off one of those women. It would be fucking suicide. Not to mention blue balls for days.

"Sure, Mack." Charlotte gave the group an apologetic smile, joining me as I waited by the door.

"Come with me," I murmured, knowing she'd follow.

"Is everything alright?"

"Yeah, just want some privacy."

She didn't argue, falling into step beside me as I reached for her hand. I held it as I climbed the stairs, going up to the second floor and down the hall to my room. I squeezed her hand and unlocked the door, gesturing for her to enter. After she entered, I shut and locked the door.

"This must be serious," she joked, placing her hand on my chest, right over my heart. "You seem a little excited. Your heart is hammering hard, big guy."

She wasn't lying. My heart *was* beating fast, but not for the reason she suspected.

Focusing on the danger surrounding her and the club, I'd grown anxious during the meeting. I couldn't let anything happen to her or Sophie. I'd never forgive myself.

"With the threat from the Outlaws and Breaker, the club is going on lockdown," I announced, more gruffly than I intended.

Charlotte blinked. "What does that mean?"

"No one leaves the compound without permission. Everyone stays inside in case of trouble."

"Are you saying I can't go to work? That Sophie can't go to school?" There was an edge to her voice, like the news annoyed her.

"Sugar," I began.

She tapped my chest. Twice. "No. I didn't just hear you tell me that you're dictating what I'm allowed to do and not do. Oh, and my daughter, too."

"It's not safe," I replied, trying to keep a hold of my temper.

I wasn't used to having my orders questioned. No one did that to the president. That disrespect was fucking serious. I had to remind myself that Charlotte didn't know this life. She didn't understand the rules. But, fuck, I wanted to spank her for this.

"Well, I guess I'm finding somewhere else to stay."

"What?" I asked, my voice so low it was a growl.

"You heard me. I'm taking Sophie somewhere else. Breaker wants to intimidate me. I'm not giving in to him. Can't you see that? I'm not going to let him intimidate me. I know to stay safe. I won't do anything stupid."

"Your place is being watched. Where will you go?"

"Right," she sighed. "I can check into a hotel for the next week. Figure it out from there. I'll use an alias. Breaker won't know where to find Sophie or me."

Did she think I wouldn't care if she left alone? Hell no.

Frowning, I shook my head. "No. Absolutely not. You can't just pack up your daughter and take her to a hotel. Everyone is here. Protection only works if you stay. Your sister knows it's the best option. Cara understands the danger and the need for lockdown."

Her hands went to her hips, and I knew I had pissed her off. "Mack Ravage, I am not a prisoner and won't be treated like one."

"Never said you were, darlin'." She caught the irritation in my voice.

"Then don't make me feel like one."

"I'm not. You're just not leaving the compound." I shrugged, not seeing the issue. "It's simple."

"Oh, it is, huh?" Her hip popped to one side as she narrowed her eyes.

Fuck me. She was goddamn gorgeous when she got fired up. The flash of her green eyes sparked a heavy lust in my loins.

"Charlotte, Sweetness, you're making this out to be something it's not."

"And if I disagree that I need to be confined to the clubhouse?" she asked, impatient for my answer.

"I might have to lock you in," I answered with conviction.

"You, you," she stammered, trying to come up with something good in response. "You big, pigheaded brute!"

What? I couldn't help my reaction. Laughter tumbled from my lips as I bent over, hardly able to contain it. "Oh, Sugar. I do love having you around."

"You're just full of opinions, aren't you?"

Her sass brought out the stubborn bull in me.

"Opinions are like assholes, Sweet Girl. Every fucking body has one."

She blinked. Twice.

The look on her face was fucking priceless. So worth sayin' that shit to her. My good girl sure had a stick up her ass when she got pissed. I loved her attempt at insulting me.

So goddamn cute.

She didn't have a harsh or mean bone in her body. Charlotte wasn't a vindictive bitch. I'd met plenty of those in my time. The curvy blonde in front of me was all sass and sweetness, and fuck if I didn't want to get her between the sheets to see if she played like this in bed.

My dick got all kinds of ideas about how I should fuck her, tie her up, and explore every inch of her body.

"Fuck, Charlotte. You turn me on."

Before she could react, I snatched her into my embrace. My lips claimed hers in a kiss that made us stumble, and I picked her up, pushing her up against the nearest wall. My hands grabbed her wrists, pinning them to the drywall above her head.

Her lower body rocked into mine as she bit my bottom lip with her teeth. Her face betrayed a mixture of annoyance and lust. "You make me crazy."

"And I turn you on," I added, licking up the side of her neck before I nibbled on the smooth skin.

"Yeah, okay," she admitted.

"Stay with me. Don't leave. I'd fucking lose my shit if something happened and I wasn't there to protect you and Sophie."

A sigh escaped her lips. "Okay, Mack."

"Seal that promise with a kiss, my sweet girl."

She lifted her chin, molding her mouth to mine.

I lost myself in the warmth of her lips, but I didn't forget the plan. Charlotte was staying put, even if I had to strap her to my bed.

Sin's Betrayal, **Ravage Riders** MC is available now.

SNEAK PEEK
TALON

I WAS IN A bad fucking mood.

Abigail had gone on three dates this week, all with the same nerdy guy with thick glasses and a stare that always rested on her ass when she wasn't looking. The ass I wanted to fucking squeeze and touch. The one I already considered *mine*. The timing sucked. Secrecy sucked.

I'd kept Crow informed and followed his instructions for eight goddamn weeks. I chased three masked men from her house on different occasions, but none of their vehicles had plates.

Not that it mattered since I sent the crows to follow. Always the same address. A pizza shop in downtown Carson City.

I scoped the place a few times while she went to work but couldn't get inside. The restaurant didn't seem to have the space for any hidden operation. Sending men to her house didn't make sense. Who the fuck wanted more information on her and why?

I sent a text to Eagle Eye.

Me:

Any news?

Eagle Eye:

Still digging

The same fucking reply I got every time I asked. He'd run financials. The owner's info. Any known affiliations. It all came back squeaky clean. And that alone raised a red flag.

No business was that legit. I knew Eagle Eye would keep working until something turned up; I just didn't have the fucking patience. I also didn't need to be blindsided by something that could get Abigail hurt.

Frowning, I almost growled as Abigail's date slipped his arm around her and led her to his car, opening the passenger door for her. She bent down to sit inside his Mustang, and he grinned like he knew he had an audience.

There go his eyes. Straight to her ass again. Fucker.

I couldn't help the churning in my gut and the worry that this could be related to the Dirty Death MC. Fucking Undertaker. Their pres caused a lot of fucking problems for our club that had nothing to do with our rivalry. He started the war with us and picked a goddamn fight when he could have left shit alone. But after he killed Rook, any hope of reaching a peaceful conclusion ended. Only his death would appease the club and our crows.

With a sigh, I scrubbed a hand down my face and over the scruff on my jaw, clenching my teeth when I saw the needle dick fucker driving Abigail to dinner.

If he touched her again, I would cut off any part of his body that dared to brush across her skin.

Mine, the crow reminded me. Yeah. I fucking heard it from him too. The crow wanted to mate. That complicated things.

My pres warned me to leave his sister alone. I should fucking listen. I intended to, but it was getting harder.

I followed the Mustang to a fucking Italian restaurant. One of those pricey ones with dark décor and romantic ambiance. He probably thought he would get lucky tonight. I'd set him straight.

I parked my bike and stalked the windows, finally stepping inside to snag a seat down the same aisle. Big menus sat on the table, and I held one up, blocking me from curious eyes.

I waited until the guy got up to take a piss, and I followed him, entering behind him as he whipped out his dick at one of the stalls.

I couldn't help glancing at it. *Yep. Needle dick.*

He could never satisfy Abigail like I could.

When he zipped up, I rushed forward, slamming his body into the wall. He yelped as I pinned him in place, checking his pockets until I pulled out his wallet.

"What the fuck? Get off me!" He wasn't much of a threat, with his face smashed into the brown tile and his arms pinned behind him.

I scanned his license, memorizing the name and address before shoving it back to where I got it. "What do you want with Abigail Holmes?"

"What?"

I repeated the question, tightening my grip.

"I-I know her from work. I like her."

With a name like Harold Simpson, I figured he probably told the truth. He sounded like a pharmacist.

"You're gonna tell her you're not feeling well and end the date."

"Why would I do that?"

"Because I will fucking chop off your cock and shove it down your goddamn throat, needle dick. She's not yours to date, touch, or even fucking think about."

"Shit," he cursed. "I don't want trouble."

"This is your only chance to avoid it. Don't ask her out again."

"Fuck. Okay, man."

"I know where you live. Remember that."

I let him go as he stumbled from the stall, rushing toward the bathroom door. He didn't even look my way.

I waited a couple of minutes before I followed, exiting the restaurant in time to catch the Mustang as it left the lot with Abigail inside. I sent the crows ahead of me as I fired up my bike, following them at a safe distance. I bet he watched that rearview mirror the entire way to Abigail's house.

A smirk twitched my lips. *Don't touch what's mine, asshole.*

Harold didn't waste time dropping her off.

The fucker didn't even make sure she got inside the house before he backed down the driveway and pressed on the gas, skidding in his haste. Abigail shook her head as she entered her home, and I parked my bike in the usual spot, cutting the engine.

Harold Simpson didn't get it. A woman like her was worth fighting over. She was perfect in every way. I noticed the organized way she arranged her clothes in her closet and cleaned the house every weekend. How she never forgot to water her plants. I trailed behind her when she went shopping, always at the same grocery store every Saturday.

She put effort into her appearance even when she only planned to buy groceries. Hair and makeup done in case one of her friends invited her to something last minute. Hell, maybe she wanted more dates. I wouldn't let it happen, but I could understand loneliness.

And that was the emotion I felt from her more than any other.

That familiar ache in the chest. A yearning for something more. We both shared it.

Later that night, with the crows watching from her roof, I slid under her bed. From here, I could feel the rise and fall of her chest like it sank into mine and slightly hovered above it. As if we shared every inhalation and exhalation, breathing in tandem. I wanted to slide out and pull back her sheets, letting her body heat and mine collide.

My eyes closed as my hands lowered, silently unbuckling my belt and popping the button on my jeans. I unzipped with such careful restraint that I nearly groaned when my cock finally sprang free. I suppressed a guttural cry of pleasure when my fist wrapped around my cock, slowly stroking the length as I imagined sliding into Abigail's pussy and that first delicious plunge inside her wet heat.

"Mmmm," she breathed above me as I heard the mattress creak.

I froze. Did she hear me?

A moan followed, and I shivered as I realized she was doing the same thing above me as I did right now. Touching herself. Getting off. Growing excited.

She needed release. Fuckkkk.

I imagined her legs falling open and her thighs parting wide. How her legs would tremble as her fingers dipped inside her tight cunt. The sticky, slick sweetness of her arousal. Was she bare? Did she leave a strip on her mound?

I needed to know. How could I have the right daydreams if I never saw her pretty pussy? Every woman in my past vanished from my head. I didn't want to imagine a single fucking thing about Abigail. I had to learn it. Memorize it. Use my teeth, lips, and tongue to map out her entire body and every inch of her skin, all the dips and valleys, every curve, the musk that settled between her legs, and the taste of her climax.

I heard a slight vibration and buzzing sound and knew what she powered on.

Naughty girl.

She might get off that way tonight, but I wouldn't let her come without me for long. The creaking of the mattress increased. Her breathy moans grew louder. I could swear her heels dug into the bed.

Fuck. I wanted her.

She fucking turned me on. Lust fogged my brain.

I kept stroking, tugging harder and faster, moving my hips only enough to cause friction. The denial collided with the need pulsing in my veins.

I knew when she came. Her soft cry echoed in the room. Not to be left behind, I followed, pumping into my fist and unable to control where I spurted as ropes of my cum landed on my stomach and shot onto the underside of her mattress. Like the sick fuck that I was, I felt satisfaction that I marked her bed with a part of me.

My body trembled with the force of that orgasm, and I knew it would be a hundred times better when I came inside her pussy. This would have to do for now.

I smeared the sticky fluid across the underside of the bed and let it dry, enjoying the thought I had claimed her in some small way. I used the bottom of my shirt to wipe myself clean and pushed my semi-hard cock back inside my pants. I needed to avoid touching myself for a bit to build up the anticipation.

Abigail's deep, even breaths soon followed. She fell asleep.

I slowly finished snapping my jeans closed and buckling my belt. I slid from under her bed, standing over her as I noted the serene expression on her face. I longed to see her sated like this after I fucked her for most of the night.

She rolled onto her side and faced me as her lips parted. I knelt at the side of her bed, toying with the idea of rubbing my thumb over the surface.

The sudden urge to lean closer and brush my lips over hers consumed me. I nearly took what I wanted but shook my head and pulled back.

I didn't want a single thing she didn't give me freely.

Forcing myself to walk out her door, I left to roam the perimeter of the house, hoping the night air would cool the heat on my skin. But it didn't stop my thoughts from focusing on the sexy woman inside. How would she taste on my tongue and feel beneath my fingertips?

The next morning, I followed her to work. I told myself I needed that energy drink and wouldn't walk by the pharmacy—a lie. I hung around in an empty aisle, watching as she cashed out customers. She always wore a smile.

Abigail never got impatient or tried to rush anyone. This woman was so fucking sweet I wondered if she should be brought into the life of a crow. Being a biker ol' lady was tough. Some women weren't cut out for it. Crow knew that firsthand. His mom split when shit got hard with the club.

But Abigail had Holmes blood. She was born into it whether Rook kept her hidden or not. And just because Crow's mother couldn't hack it, it didn't mean the same for Abigail. It sure got me curious about what kind of life she had before now. How was it possible she never learned about her brother or the motorcycle club that meant everything to her father?

I checked out at the front of the store and headed to my bike, chugging the energy drink before I rode out of the lot. My head was a fuckin' mess, and I went for a ride to clear it, arriving an hour before her shift was scheduled to end.

That night, I stayed outside and didn't enter the house. I had to get this possessive urge to claim her out of my system. Crow would fucking kill me if he knew how far I had gone already, testing the limits and pushing boundaries.

I had it under control. . .until ten days later when everything went to shit.

Talon, **Devil's Murder MC** is available now.

ABOUT THE AUTHOR

Nikki Landis is a romance enthusiast, tea addict, and book hoarder. She's the USA Today Bestselling Author of over fifty novels, including her widely popular Tonopah, NV RBMC series. She writes wickedly fierce, spicy romances featuring dirty talkin' bikers, deadly, overprotective reapers, wild bad boys, and the feisty, independent women they love. She's a mom to six sons, two of them Marines. Books are her favorite escape.

Nikki writes sci-fi and monster romance under the pen name Synna Star. She lives in Ohio with her husband, boys, and a little Yorkie who really runs the whole house.

Made in the USA
Las Vegas, NV
18 August 2024

94017977R00116